MAIGRET'S MISTAKE

Georges

MAIGRET'S

Simenon

MISTAKE

Translated from the French by Alan Hodge

A Harvest/HBJ Book
A Helen and Kurt Wolff Book
Harcourt Brace Jovanovich, Publishers
San Diego   New York   London

Copyright 1953 by Georges Simenon
Copyright renewed 1981 by Georges Simenon
All rights reserved. No part of this publication may be
reproduced or transmitted in any form or by any means,
electronic or mechanical, including photocopy, recording,
or any information storage and retrieval system, without
permission in writing from the publisher.

Requests for permission to make copies of any
part of the work should be mailed to:
Permissions, Harcourt Brace Jovanovich, Publishers,
Orlando, Florida 32887.

Library of Congress Cataloging-in-Publication Data
Simenon, Georges, 1903–
[Maigret se trompe. English]
Maigret's mistake/by Georges Simenon: translated by
Alan Hodge.
p.   cm.
Translation of: Maigret se trompe.
"A Harvest/HBJ book."
"A Helen and Kurt Wolff book."
ISBN 0-15-655155-1 (pbk.)
I. Title.
PQ2637.I53M28413   1988
843'.912—dc19   88-970

Printed in the United States of America

First Harvest/HBJ edition 1988

A B C D E F G H I J

MAIGRET'S MISTAKE

1

I T was eight-twenty-five in the morning when Maigret rose from the breakfast-table still drinking his last cup of coffee. Though it was only November, the lights were on. At the window, Madame Maigret was peering through the fog at the passers-by, who were hurrying to work, shoulders hunched and hands in pockets.

'You'd better put on your heavy overcoat,' she said.

For it was by watching people in the street that she decided what the weather was like. This morning, everyone was walking fast and many wore scarves; they had a particular way of stamping along the pavement to warm their feet, and she had noticed several blowing their noses.

'I'll go and get it for you.'

He was still holding his cup in his hand when the telephone bell echoed through the house.

Picking up the receiver, he too looked outside; the houses opposite were almost hidden by the yellowish mist that had overnight filled the streets.

'Hello! Inspector Maigret? . . . Dupeu speaking from the Quartier des Ternes. . . .'

It was odd that it should be Inspector Dupeu, for he was the man who probably had most in common with the atmosphere of that day. Dupeu was Inspector of Police in the Rue d'Etoile. He squinted. His wife squinted. And it was said that all three of his daughters, whom Maigret had never seen, squinted too. He was a conscientious official, so bothered about doing his best that he practically made himself ill by it. Even inanimate objects seemed peculiarly dreary when he was present, and in spite of the fact that he was the best fellow in the world, one could not help trying to avoid him. Besides, summer and winter, he had a perpetual cold.

'Sorry to trouble you at home. I thought you wouldn't have left yet, and so I said to myself . . .'

There was nothing to do but be patient. Dupeu had to explain himself. Invariably he felt obliged to recount at length why he did this or that, as if he were in the wrong.

'. . . I know you like to be on the spot in person. I may be mistaken, but I have an idea that we are on to a pretty interesting affair. Bear in mind that I don't know anything yet, or hardly anything. I have only just arrived.'

Madame Maigret was waiting with the overcoat in her arms, and, so that she would not grow impatient, her husband whispered to her:

'Dupeu!'

Meanwhile Dupeu droned on.

'As I usually do, I reached the office at eight o'clock and I was looking through the first post, when at eight-seven I had a telephone call from the charwoman. It was she who found the body when she entered the flat in the Avenue Carnot. As it's almost next door, I hurried round with my secretary.'

'Murder?'

'Strictly, it could be suicide, but I'm convinced it's murder.'

'Who is it?'

'A certain Louise Filon. I've never heard of her. A young woman.'

'I'll be along.'

Dupeu started speaking again, but Maigret, pretending not to notice, had already hung up. Before leaving, he called the Quai des Orfèvres and had himself put through to the *Identité Judiciaire*.

'Is Moers there? Yes, call him to the telephone. Hello! Is that you, Moers? Will you come along with your men to the Avenue Carnot? . . . Murder . . . I shall be there. . . .'

He gave him the number of the block, put on his coat, and, a few seconds later, one more dim outline was hastening through the fog. Not until the corner of the Boulevard Voltaire did he find a taxi.

Around the Etoile, the avenues were almost

deserted. Men were collecting dustbins. For the most part, curtains were still drawn, and only in a few windows was a light to be seen.

In the Avenue Carnot, a policeman in a cape was standing on the pavement, but there were no onlookers and no crowd.

'What floor?' Maigret asked.

'The third.'

He went through the main door, ornamented with highly polished brass knobs. In the porter's lodge, where the lights were on, the concierge was eating breakfast. She watched him through the window, but did not get up. The lift worked noiselessly, as in every well-kept house. The carpets, on the waxed oak of the staircase, were of a deep red.

On the third floor he was confronted with three doors; as he paused, the one on the left opened. Dupeu was there, his nose red, as Maigret had expected.

'Come in. I decided not to touch anything while I was waiting for you. I haven't even questioned the charwoman.'

Crossing the hall, which contained only a coat-rack and two chairs, they entered the sitting-room, where the lights were on.

'The charwoman was at once struck by the lights being on.'

In the corner of a yellow sofa sprawled a young woman with brown hair, curiously doubled over herself. A big dark red stain marked her dressing-gown.

'She was hit by a bullet in the head. It seems

to have been fired from behind, and from very close quarters. As you can see, she didn't fall down.'

She had simply collapsed to the right, and her head hung down, the hair almost touching the carpet.

'Where is the charwoman?'

'In the kitchen. She asked permission to make a cup of coffee. According to her, she arrived at eight, as she does every morning. She has a key to the flat. She came in, saw the body, claims that she touched nothing and telephoned me at once.'

Only then did Maigret appreciate what had struck him as so odd when he had first arrived. Generally on the pavement he would have had to make his way through a row of spectators. Usually, too, the other tenants are on the lookout on the landings. But here, all was as quiet as if nothing had happened.

'Is the kitchen this way?'

He found it at the end of a corridor. The door was open. A woman in a black dress, and with dark hair and eyes, was sitting near the gas stove, drinking a cup of coffee and blowing on it to cool it.

Maigret had an idea that he had seen her before. He observed her, frowning, while she steadily returned his gaze, still drinking coffee. She was very small. Sitting down, she could scarcely touch the floor with her feet; she was wearing shoes too big for her and her dress was too full and too long.

'I think we have met before,' he said.

Self-possessed, she replied:

'It's very likely.'

'What is your name?'

'Désirée Brault.'

The Christian name gave him a clue.

'Weren't you once arrested for shoplifting in one of the big stores?'

'That among other things.'

'What else?'

'I've been arrested so many times!'

Her face showed no fear. In fact, it showed nothing. She looked at him. She answered him. But what she was thinking it was impossible to guess.

'You've done time?'

'You'll find all that in my record.'

'Prostitution?'

'Why not?'

A long time ago, obviously. Now she would be fifty or sixty. She was wizened. Her hair had not turned white or even grey, but it was sparse, and through it you could see her scalp.

'There was a time when I was as good as the next girl!'

'How long have you been working in this flat?'

'A year next month. I began in December, not long before the holidays.'

'Do you work here all day?'

'Only from eight till twelve.'

The coffee smelt so good that Maigret helped himself to a cup. Inspector Dupeu was standing timidly in the doorway.

'Would you like a cup, Dupeu?'

'No, thank you. I had breakfast less than half an hour ago.'

Désirée Brault got up to pour a second cup for herself as well, and her dress hung loosely round her. She could not have weighed more than a little girl of fourteen.

'You have other jobs?'

'Three or four. It depends on the weeks.'

'You live alone?'

'With my husband.'

'Has he done time, too?'

'Not likely! He keeps to the drink.'

'Has he no job?'

'He's never done a stroke of work in fifteen years, not even to hammer a nail in the wall.'

She spoke without bitterness, in level tones in which it was hard to detect any irony.

'What happened this morning?'

She nodded at Dupeu.

'Didn't he tell you? All right. I got here at eight o'clock.'

'Where do you live?'

'Near the Place Clichy. I took the Metro. I opened the door with my key and I noticed a light in the sitting-room.'

'The sitting-room door was open?'

'No.'

'Is your employer usually up by the time you arrive in the morning?'

'She didn't get up till about ten, and sometimes later.'

'What did she do?'

7

'Nothing.'

'Go on.'

'I opened the sitting-room door and I saw her.'

'You didn't touch her?'

'I didn't need to, to see that she was dead. Have you ever seen anyone walking about with half her face blown off?'

'And then?'

'I called the police.'

'Without arousing the neighbours, or the concierge?'

She shrugged her shoulders.

'Why should I?'

'But after you telephoned?'

'I waited.'

'Doing what?'

'Doing nothing.'

It was astonishing, this artlessness. She had simply stayed there, waiting until someone rang the door-bell, perhaps gazing at the corpse.

'You're sure you didn't touch anything?'

'Of course I didn't.'

'Did you find a revolver?'

'I found nothing at all.'

Inspector Dupeu interrupted:

'We have looked everywhere for the weapon, but without success.'

'Did Louise Filon own a revolver?'

'If she did, I never saw it.'

'Is any of the furniture kept locked up?'

'No.'

'I suppose you know what these cupboards contain?'

'Yes.'

'And you have never seen a gun?'

'Never.'

'Tell me, did your employer know that you had been in prison?'

'I told her everything.'

'It didn't frighten her?'

'It amused her. I don't know whether she had done time, too, but she might have.'

'What do you mean?'

'That before she came to live here she was on the streets.'

'How do you know?'

'Because she told me. And even if she hadn't . . .'

Footsteps were heard on the landing and Dupeu went to open the door. It was Moers and his men with their gear. Maigret said to Moers:

'Don't begin just yet. And while you're waiting for me, telephone the Public Prosecutor.'

He was fascinated by Désirée Brault and by everything he guessed to lie behind her words. He took off his overcoat, for it was warm, sat down and sipped his coffee.

'Sit down.'

'Kind of you. It's not often charwomen have that said to them.'

And for once she almost smiled.

'Have you any idea who might have killed your employer?'

'Certainly not.'

'Did she have many callers?'

'I never saw anyone, except the local doctor

once when she had bronchitis. But of course I leave at twelve o'clock.'

'You don't know if she had any friends?'

'All I know is that there are some men's slippers and a man's dressing-gown in a wardrobe. Also a box of cigars. She didn't smoke cigars.'

'You've no idea who the man was?'

'I've never seen him.'

'You don't know his name? He never telephoned when you were here?'

'That did happen.'

'What did she call him?'

'Pierrot.'

'Somebody kept her?'

'I suppose somebody had to pay the rent, and all the rest of it, don't you?'

Maigret got to his feet, set down his cup and filled his pipe.

'What do you want me to do?' she asked.

'Nothing. You just wait.'

He returned to the sitting-room where the men of the *Identité Judiciaire* were waiting for his orders before falling to work. The room was perfectly tidy. In an ash-tray near the sofa was some cigarette-ash, and the butts of three cigarettes, two of them marked with lip-stick.

A half-open door led into the bedroom where Maigret noted with some surprise that the bed was unmade, the pillow dented as if someone had slept there.

'Hasn't the doctor come?'

'He wasn't at home. His wife is trying to reach

him at the homes of patients he is to see this morning.'

He opened a number of cupboards and drawers. Clothes and underclothes were those of a girl who dressed with rather poor taste and not those one expected to find in a flat in the Avenue Carnot.

'Look after the fingerprints and the rest of it, Moers. I am going down to talk to the concierge.'

Inspector Dupeu asked him:

'Do you need me any more?'

'No, thank you. Send me your report in the course of the day. It's been very kind of you, Dupeu.'

'Well, I thought at once that this would interest you. If there had been a weapon near the sofa, I should have concluded that it was suicide, for the shot seems to have been fired point-blank. Although women of this sort generally kill themselves with veronal. It's at least five years since I have known any woman in this district kill herself with a revolver. Therefore, as long as there was no weapon . . .'

'Dupeu, you've done a fine job. . . .'

'I try to the best of my ability to. . . .'

He talked on all the way down the staircase. Maigret left him on the mat outside the porter's lodge, and went in.

'Good morning, madame.'

'Good morning, Inspector.'

'You know who I am?'

She nodded that she did.

'You are aware of what has happened?'

'I asked the policeman on duty on the pavement. He told me that Mademoiselle Louise is dead.'

The porter's lodge had the middle-class look of all the lodges in the district. The concierge, who was only in her forties, was well dressed, and even smartly so. She was rather attractive, though her features were slightly overblown.

'Has she been murdered?' she asked, as Maigret sat down near the window.

'Why do you think that?'

'I suppose if she'd died a natural death, the police wouldn't be here.'

'She might have committed suicide.'

'That wouldn't have been like her.'

'You knew her well?'

'Not very well. She never spent much time down here. She just opened the door to ask for her mail. She never felt herself at home, you know, in this house.'

'You mean to say that she wasn't of the same class as the other tenants?'

'Yes.'

'What class do you think she belonged to?'

'I don't quite know. I've no reason to run her down. She was a quiet creature, and didn't give herself airs.'

'Her charwoman never said anything?'

'Madame Brault and I don't speak to each other.'

'But you know her?'

'I don't care to. I've seen her come and go. That is enough.'

'Was Louise Filon a kept woman?'

'It could be. But, in any case, she paid her rent regularly.'

'Did she have visitors?'

'From time to time.'

'Not regularly?'

'No, it couldn't be called regularly.'

Maigret thought he sensed a reticence. Unlike Madame Brault, the concierge was nervous, and now and again she cast a quick glance through the glass door. It was she who observed:

'The doctor's going up.'

'Tell me, Madame . . . by the way, what is your name?'

'Cornet.'

'Tell me, Madame Cornet, is there something you'd like to keep from me?'

She did her best to look him straight in the eye.

'Why do you ask that?'

'No reason. I just like to know. Was it always the same man who came to see Louise Filon?'

'It was always the same one I saw.'

'What sort of a man?'

'A musician.'

'How do you know he was a musician?'

'Because once or twice I saw him carrying a saxophone-case.'

'Did he call yesterday evening?'

'About ten o'clock, yes.'

'Did you let him in and out?'

'No. Until I go to bed, about eleven, I leave the door open.'

'But you can see who is passing through the hall?'

'Mostly, yes. The tenants are a quiet lot. Nearly all are people of standing.'

'You say that this musician went upstairs about ten o'clock?'

'Yes. He didn't stay more than ten minutes. When he left he seemed to be in a great hurry, and I heard him rushing towards the Etoile.'

'Did you notice his expression? Did he seem excited? . . .'

'No.'

'That night did Louise Filon have any other visitors?'

'No.'

'So that if the doctor finds that the crime was committed between ten o'clock and eleven, it is almost certain that . . .'

'I didn't say that. I only said that he was her only visitor.'

'According to you, the musician was her lover?'

She did not at once reply. Eventually she muttered:

'I don't know.'

'What do you mean?'

'Nothing. I was just thinking about the rent of the flat.'

'I see. He wasn't the kind of musician who could keep a girl-friend in a flat like that?'

'That's it.'

'You don't seem to be surprised, Madame Cornet, that your tenant should have been murdered.'

'It's not a thing I expected, but I'm not much surprised either.'

'Why not?'

'For no real reason. I rather think that women of this sort run greater risks than others. At any rate, that's the idea you get from reading the newspapers.'

'I should like to ask you for a list of all the tenants who came in or went out after nine o'clock yesterday evening. I shall pick it up when I go.'

'Very good.'

When he left the lodge he met the prosecutor and his deputy getting out of their car, along with their clerk. All three seemed to be feeling the cold. The fog had not yet dispersed, and the steam of their breath was blowing into it.

They shook hands, and took the lift. With the exception of the third floor, the whole block was as quiet as when Maigret had arrived. People here were not the sort to spy on comings and goings through half-open doors, nor to gather in a crowd on the landings because a woman had been murdered.

Almost all over the flat, Moers and his men had set up their technical apparatus, and the doctor had finished examining the body. He clasped Maigret's hand.

'About what time?' the inspector asked.

'At first sight, between nine in the evening

and midnight. Eleven o'clock, perhaps, rather than midnight.'

'I suppose death was instantaneous?'

'You've seen the body. The shot was fired point-blank.'

'From behind?'

'From behind, but a little from one side.'

Moers interrupted:

'At that moment she must have been smoking a cigarette, which fell on the carpet and burnt itself out. It was lucky that the carpet didn't catch fire.'

'What exactly is the case?' asked the deputy prosecutor, who was still in the dark.

'I don't know. It may be a commonplace murder. But that would surprise me.'

'You have a clue?'

'None at all. I am going to talk to the charwoman again.'

Before making for the kitchen, he telephoned the Quai des Orfèvres, and asked Lucas, who was on duty, to join him at once. After that, he took no further notice of the prosecutor and his staff, nor of the police technicians who were carrying on with their usual jobs.

Madame Brault was sitting in the same place. She had stopped drinking coffee, but was smoking a cigarette, which went oddly with her tiny figure.

'I suppose I may?' she asked, following Maigret's glance.

He sat down facing her.

'Out with it.'

'Out with what?'

'Everything you know.'

'I've told you already.'

'How did Louise Filon spend her time?'

'I can only speak for what she did in the mornings. She got up at about ten o'clock, or rather she woke then, but didn't get up at once. I used to bring her coffee and she drank it in bed while she read and smoked.'

'What did she read?'

'Magazines and novels. She also often listened to the radio. You must have noticed that there's a set on the bedside table.'

'She didn't telephone anyone?'

'About eleven.'

'Every day?'

'Nearly every day.'

'Pierrot?'

'Yes. Sometimes about noon she dressed to go out and eat, but that wasn't very often. Most days she sent me down to the delicatessen to fetch cold meat and made-up dishes.'

'You don't know what she did with her afternoons?'

'I suppose she went out. She must have done, because every morning her shoes were dirty. I expect she hung around the shops as all women do.'

'She didn't have dinner at home?'

'There were seldom any dirty dishes.'

'She went out to meet Pierrot?'

'Him or somebody else.'

'You're sure you've never seen him?'

'Quite sure.'

'You've never seen any other man here either?'

'Only the gas-man or a delivery boy.'

'How long is it since you came out of prison?'

'Six years.'

'Have you lost the itch to go shoplifting?'

'I don't have the right looks any more. . . . They're just taking the body away.'

A noise could be heard in the sitting-room, and it was in fact the men from the *Institut Médico-Légal*.

'She didn't enjoy it for long!'

'What do you mean?'

'She had a wretched life until she was twenty-four, and then she hardly had more than two years in the good.'

'She confided in you?'

'We talked like human beings.'

'Did she tell you where she came from?'

'She was born in the XVIIIth *arrondissement*, practically in the gutter. She spent most of her life in the Chapelle district. When she moved in here, she thought she was in for a lovely life.'

'She wasn't happy?'

The charwoman shrugged her shoulders and gave Maigret a pitying glance, as if she were surprised to find him so lacking in understanding.

'Do you think it was fun for her to live in a house like this, where people wouldn't condescend to look at her when they passed her on the stairs?'

'Why did she come here?'

'She must have had her reasons.'

'Was it her musician who kept her?'

'Who's been talking about a musician?'

'Never mind. Pierrot is a saxophonist?'

'I think so. I know that he plays in a dance-hall.'

She said only what she chose to tell. Now that Maigret had a slightly clearer idea of the sort of girl Louise Filon was, he was convinced that the two women had spent their mornings chattering freely to one another.

'I do not think,' he said, 'that a dance-band musician could have been in a position to pay the rent of a flat like this.'

'Nor do I.'

'So?'

'So there must have been someone else,' she admitted calmly.

'Pierrot came to see her yesterday evening.'

She showed no surprise, but kept looking him straight in the eye.

'I suppose you decided straight off that it was he who killed her? There's only one thing I can tell you: they were very much in love.'

'She told you so?'

'Not only were they in love, but their one thought was to get married.'

'Why didn't they?'

'Perhaps because they had no money. Perhaps because the other one wouldn't let her go.'

'The other one?'

'You know as well as I do that I mean the man who paid the rent. Do I have to draw a diagram?'

A thought came to Maigret and he went into the bedroom and opened the cupboard. He pulled out a pair of men's slippers in glacé kid, made to measure by a boot-maker in the Rue Saint-Honoré who was one of the most exclusive in Paris. Taking the heavy silk dressing-gown down from the peg, he observed the label of a shirt-maker in the Rue de Rivoli.

Moers's men had already left. Moers himself was waiting for Maigret in the sitting-room.

'What have you discovered?'

'Finger-prints, of course, both old and new.'

'A man's?'

'One man's, at least. We shall have them developed within the hour.'

'Send them to the Index Office. You may take away these slippers and the dressing-gown. At the Quai, hand them over to Janvier or Torrence. I should like them to be shown to the shops where they were bought.'

'The slippers will be easy, I think; they're marked with the maker's number.'

Once more quiet enveloped the flat, and Maigret went to look for the charwoman in the kitchen.

'You needn't stay any longer.'

'Can I clean up?'

'Not today.'

'What shall I do?'

'You may go home. But you are forbidden to leave Paris. It may be . . .'

'I understand.'

'You're sure you've nothing more to tell me?'

'If I remember anything else, I'll let you know.'

'One more question. You're sure that from the moment you found the body to the moment the police arrived, you never left the flat?'

'I'll take my oath.'

'And nobody called?'

'Not even a cat.'

She unhooked her shopping bag, which she probably always carried with her, and Maigret made certain that it held no revolver.

'You can search me, if you wish.'

He did not search her, but for conscience' sake, and not without feeling embarrassed by it, he ran his hands over her baggy dress.

'Once upon a time you might have enjoyed doing that!'

She took her leave, and on the stairs must have passed Lucas, whose hat and coat were wet.

'Raining?'

'For the past ten minutes. What shall I do, Chief?'

'I don't know exactly. I should like you to stay here. If anyone telephones, try to find out where the call is coming from. It may be that someone will ring at about eleven. Tell the office to tap the wire. As for the rest, just make a thorough search. It's been done already, but one never knows.'

'What's it all about exactly?'

'A prostitute who had her beat in the Barbès

district. Someone set her up here. So far as we can tell, she had a dance-band player for a steady lover.'

'Did he kill her?'

'He came to see her last night. The concierge declares that nobody else went up.'

'Have you a description of him?'

'I am just going down to interview the concierge again.'

The concierge was busily sorting out the second post. According to her, Pierrot was a young man of about thirty, fair and thickset, who looked more like a butcher's apprentice than a musician.

'You've nothing else to tell me?'

'Nothing, Monsieur Maigret. If I remember anything I shall let you know.'

It was strange. Almost the same reply as the charwoman had given. Maigret was certain that both of them, doubtless for different reasons, were trying to avoid telling him all they knew.

As he would indubitably have to walk as far as the Etoile before finding a taxi, he put up his overcoat collar and set off, hands in pockets, just like the people whom Madame Maigret had watched from the window that morning. The fog had turned into a fine cold rain which put him in mind of a cold in the head, and at the corner of the street he stopped at a bar to drink a hot toddy.

2

JANVIER was the one who checked up on the man named Pierrot, and reconstructed his actions and movements up to the moment when the musician had chosen to vanish.

A little before eleven-thirty, Lucas, who was quietly ferreting about in the flat in the Avenue Carnot, had at last heard the telephone ring. He lifted the receiver, taking care to say nothing. At the other end a man's voice had murmured:

'Is that you?'

Before he grew suspicious of the silence that greeted him, Pierrot had added:

'You aren't alone?'

And then anxiously:

'Hello! Is that Carnot 22–35?'

'Carnot 22–35. Yes.'

Over the telephone Lucas could hear the man's breathing. He was calling from a public booth,

23

probably in a bar, for there had been the characteristic noise of a telephone-token falling in the metal box.

After a moment, the musician hung up. Lucas had merely to wait for a call from the official at the switch-board. This took hardly a couple of minutes.

'Lucas? Your man was calling from a *bistrot* on the Boulevard Rochechouart, at the corner of the Rue Riquet. Its name is Chez Léon.'

Lucas immediately telephoned the police station in the Goutte d'Or district, a few steps from the Boulevard Rochechouart.

'May I speak to Inspector Janin?'

As it happened, he was in the office. Lucas gave him a rough description of Pierrot and told him the name of the bar.

'Don't do anything until Janvier joins you.'

Then he got Janvier on the line. Meanwhile the rain was still falling on a world of brick, stone and concrete, through which dark shadows with umbrellas flitted by. Maigret was in his office, his collar undone and four stuffed pipes set before him, finishing off an administrative report that had to be delivered by midday. Janvier pushed the office door half-open.

'He's telephoned, sir. We know where he is. Lucas has warned the Goutte d'Or district and Janin ought to be on the spot already. I'm pushing down there now. What shall I do with him?'

The inspector looked up with heavy tired eyes.

'Bring him to me, gently.'

'Are you going out to lunch?'

'I shall have sandwiches sent up.'

Janvier used one of the little black P.J. cars which he stopped some distance away from the bar. The *bistrot* was long and narrow, with so much steam on the windows that it was impossible to see inside. When he opened the door, he saw Janin waiting for him, drinking a *vermouth-cassis*. There were only four other customers. The tiled floor was covered with sawdust, the walls were a dirty yellow, and the telephone booth stood by the wash-rooms.

'Has he gone?'

Janin, as he shook hands, nodded yes. The proprietor, who must have known the local policeman, asked Janvier in slightly ironical tones:

'Have a drink?'

'A *bock*.'

The customers were watching them. Janin must have already interrogated them.

'It's safe to talk,' he said in a low voice. 'He came in at ten-forty-five, as he usually does.'

'Does the proprietor know his name?'

'He only knows that he's called Pierrot; that he's a musician and must live in the neighbourhood. Every morning he comes in here at ten-forty-five to have his coffee. Generally, at eleven o'clock he has a telephone call. This morning nobody called him. He waited half an hour and then went into the booth. When he came out he looked worried. He paused for a moment at the bar; then he paid and left.'

'Do they know where he has his lunch?'

'The proprietor claims he doesn't know. Do you need me any more?'

'I don't know. Let's go.'

Outside, Janvier glanced up the Rue Riquet; it was a very short street in which hung signs of two hotels that probably let rooms by the hour.

If it was Pierrot's habit to take his morning coffee in this bar, it was likely that he lived just around the corner.

'Shall we go and see?'

The first lodging-house was called the Hotel du Var. To the right of the corridor was an office, and in it an old woman.

'Is Pierrot in?'

Janin, who would be well known to her, took care not to show himself and Janvier, of all the officers in the P.J., looked least like a policeman.

'It's more than an hour since he went out.'

'You're sure he hasn't come back?'

'Quite sure. I haven't stirred from the office. Besides, his key's on the rack.'

Suddenly she caught sight of Janin who had stepped forward a few paces.

'Oh! That's it, is it? What do you want with the boy?'

'Hand me the register. How long has he been living here?'

'More than a year. He rents a room by the month.'

She reached for the register and turned over the pages.

'Look. This house is above board.'

Pierrot's real name was Pierre Eyraud; he was twenty-nine and born in Paris.

'What time does he usually come in?'

'Sometimes he comes back in the early afternoon. Sometimes not.'

'Does he bring women in with him?'

'They all do.'

'Always the same girl?'

She did not hold back for long. She knew that if she did not toe the line, Janin would find a hundred opportunities for making trouble for her.

'You must know her, Monsieur Janin. She hung about this district long enough. It's Lulu.'

'Lulu who?'

'I don't know. I've always called her Lulu. A nice girl, and she's struck it lucky. Now she has fur coats and all, and comes in a taxi.'

Janvier inquired:

'Did you see her yesterday?'

'No, not yesterday; the day before. That was Sunday, wasn't it? She arrived just before midday with some small parcels and they had lunch upstairs. Later they went out arm in arm—to the cinema, I suppose.'

'Give me the key.'

She shrugged her shoulders. Refusing would do no good.

'Do your best so that he won't notice you've searched his room. He'd blame it on me.'

By way of precaution, Janin stayed downstairs; among other things, to stop the old woman from telephoning Pierre Eyraud and giving him the news. All the doors were open on the first floor, which contained the rooms hired for an hour or for less. Higher up, the weekly and monthly tenants lived, and various noises could be heard from behind their doors; evidently there was another musician in the hotel, for someone was playing an accordion.

Janvier reached number 53, which looked out on the courtyard. The bed was an iron one, and the rug worn and faded, as was the table-cover. On the wash-stand lay a toothbrush, a tube of toothpaste, a comb, a shaving-brush and a razor. A large, unlocked suitcase in a corner served as a receptacle for dirty linen.

In the cupboard Janvier found only one suit, an old pair of trousers, a grey felt hat and a cap. As for Pierrot's linen, it consisted solely of three or four shirts, some pairs of socks and underpants. Another drawer was filled with sheets of music. From the lower shelf of the bedside-table he unearthed a pair of women's bedroom slippers, and, hanging behind the door, a dressing-gown in salmon-pink crêpe-de-chine.

By the time he came downstairs, Janin had had a chat with the landlady.

'I've got the address of two or three restaurants where he usually eats his lunch, sometimes in one, sometimes in another.'

Janvier took no notice until they were in the street.

'You had better stay here,' he told Janin. 'When the evening papers are on the streets, he will find out what has happened to his girl-friend, if he doesn't know it already. Perhaps he will drop in at the hotel.'

'You think he did it?'

'The boss has told me nothing.'

Janvier set off first for an Italian restaurant on the Boulevard Rochechouart; a quiet comfortable place which smelt of highly seasoned cooking. Two waitresses in black and white hustled around the tables, but nobody answered to Pierrot's description.

'Have you seen Pierre Eyraud?'

'The musician? No. He hasn't appeared. What day is it? Tuesday? I should be surprised if he did come; it isn't his day.'

The second restaurant on the list was a brasserie near the Barbès crossroads; nobody there had seen Pierrot, either.

The last chance remained; it was a drivers' café, painted yellow outside, and with a bill of fare chalked on a slate hanging on the door. The proprietor was behind the counter, pouring out wine. One young girl, tall and thin, was the only waitress, and the proprietor's wife could be seen in the kitchen.

Janvier approached the zinc-topped bar and asked for a *bock*; the customers must all have been regulars, for they watched him with curiosity.

'I have no draught beer,' the proprietor said. 'Won't you have a glass of Beaujolais?'

Janvier nodded, and paused a few moments before he asked:

'Has Pierrot been in?'

'The musician?'

'Yes. He made an appointment with me here for twelve-fifteen.'

It was twelve-forty-five.

'If you'd come at twelve-fifteen, you would have found him.'

They were unsuspecting; for Janvier's attitude seemed quite straightforward.

'He didn't wait for me?'

'To tell you the truth, he didn't even finish his lunch.'

'Someone came to fetch him?'

'No. He left suddenly, saying he was in a hurry.'

'What time was that?'

'About a quarter of an hour ago.'

Janvier, who was glancing round the tables, noticed that two of the customers were reading the afternoon papers over their lunch. One table near the window had not yet been cleared. There, by the side of a plate of veal stew, a paper lay spread out.

'He was sitting there?'

'Yes.'

Janvier had some two hundred yards to walk through the rain in order to join Janin, who was on duty in the Rue Riquet.

'Has he returned?'

'I've seen no one.'

'Less than half an hour ago, he was sitting in a little restaurant. A newspaper-seller passed by, and as soon as he caught a glimpse of the front page, he rushed away. I had better telephone the boss.'

At the Quai des Orfèvres, a tray stood on Maigret's desk bearing two huge sandwiches and two bottles of beer. The inspector listened to Janvier's report.

'Try to find out the name of the dance-hall where he works. His landlady probably knows it. It must be somewhere in the district. Tell Janin to continue watching the hotel.'

Maigret was right. The landlady knew. She, too, had a newspaper in her office but she had not connected the Louise Filon of the headlines with the Lulu whom she knew. In any case, all the paper said in its first edition was:

A certain Louise Filon, of no profession, was found dead this morning by her charwoman in a flat in the Avenue Carnot. She had been killed by a revolver bullet fired at point-blank range, probably yesterday evening. Robbery does not seem to have been the motive for the murder. Inspector Maigret is personally conducting the investigation, and we understand that he is already following a promising line of inquiry.

Pierrot worked at the Grelot, a dance-hall in the Rue Charbonnière, almost on the corner of the Boulevard de la Chapelle. It was in the same district, but in the least savoury part of it. As soon as he reached the Boulevard de la Chapelle, Janvier came upon Arabs wandering about in the rain, looking as if they had nothing to do. Besides the Arabs, there were other men, and women too, hanging about in broad daylight and, in spite of the regulations, waiting to pick up customers on the steps of the hotels.

The front of the Grelot was painted mauve, and in the evenings its lighting was evidently also mauve. At this time of day, no one was to be seen inside except the proprietor, engaged at lunch with a middle-aged woman who may have been his wife. He scrutinized Janvier, who had shut the door behind him, and Janvier sensed that the man at first glance had guessed his profession.

'What do you want? The bar doesn't open until five.'

Janvier displayed his badge, and the proprietor didn't move a muscle. He was short and broad, with the nose and ears of an ex-boxer. Above the dance-floor there hung from the wall a sort of balcony to which the band had to climb by a ladder.

'Well, then?'

'Is Pierrot here?'

The proprietor gazed round the empty room, and said no more than:

'Can you see him?'

'He hasn't been here today?'

'He doesn't start work in the evenings until seven o'clock. Sometimes he looks in at four or five o'clock for a game of *belote*.'

'Was he at work yesterday?'

Janvier at once saw that he was on to something, for the man and woman had exchanged glances.

'What has he done?' the proprietor cautiously asked.

'Perhaps nothing. I just have one or two questions to put to him.'

'Why?'

The inspector staked all on one throw.

'Because Lulu is dead.'

'What? What are you saying?'

He was genuinely surprised. And there was no newspaper in sight.

'When did she die?'

'Last night.'

'What happened to her?'

'Did you know her?'

'There was a time when she used to be a regular. She was here nearly every night. I mean about two years ago.'

'But since then?'

'She came from time to time, for a drink and to listen to the band.'

'What time yesterday evening did Pierrot take time off?'

'Who told you he'd taken time off?'

'The concierge at the Avenue Carnot, who knows him well, saw him enter the block, and leave again a quarter of an hour later.'

The proprietor was silent for a full minute, making up his mind what line to take. He, too, was at the mercy of the police.

'Tell me first what happened to Lulu.'

'She's been murdered.'

'Not by Pierrot!' he retorted emphatically.

'I didn't say it was by Pierrot.'

'Then what do you want with him?'

'I need certain information. You maintain that he worked here last night?'

'I maintain nothing. It's the truth. At seven o'clock he was up there playing his saxophone.'

With a glance he indicated the hanging platform.

'But about nine o'clock he left?'

'He had a telephone call. It was nine-twenty.'

'From Lulu?'

'I don't know, but very likely.'

'I do know,' his wife said. 'I was near the telephone.'

The telephone was not in a booth, but in a recess in the wall, next to the wash-room door.

'He told her:

' "I'll be round at once."

'Then he turned to me:

' "Mélanie, I simply must slip round there."

'I asked him:

' "Something wrong?"

'He answered:

' "It seems so."

'And he climbed up to speak to the rest of the band before rushing out.'

'What time did he come back?'

It was the man's turn to reply:

'A little before eleven.'

'Did he seem excited?'

'I didn't notice. He apologized for his absence and went back to his place. He played until one in the morning. Then, as usual after closing-time, he had a drink with us. If he had known that Lulu was dead, he would never have had the nerve to do that. He was crazy about her. And it didn't date from yesterday. Many a time I've told him:

' "Pierrot, my boy, you're making a mistake. You have to take women for what they're worth and . . ." '

His wife interrupted him dryly:

'Thanks?'

'Ah, that's not the same thing at all.'

'Lulu wasn't in love with him?'

'Of course she was.'

'But she had another man, too?'

'A saxophonist couldn't keep her in a flat in the Etoile district.'

'Do you know who he was?'

'She never told me, nor did Pierrot. All I know is that her life changed after her operation.'

'What operation?'

'Two years ago she was taken very ill. She lived round here then.'

'She walked the streets?'

The man shrugged his shoulders:

'What else do they do round here?'

'Go on.'

'She was taken to hospital, and when Pierrot came back from seeing her, he said there was no hope. It was something to do with her head, I don't know what. Two days later, they took her to another hospital on the Left Bank. They performed God knows what operation on her, and in a few weeks she was cured. Only she never came back to these parts afterwards, except on a visit.'

'So she set up immediately in the Avenue Carnot?'

'Can you remember?' the proprietor asked his wife.

'Yes, I do. At first she had a flat in the Rue La Fayette.'

When Janvier returned to the Quai des Orfèvres, about three o'clock, he knew nothing more. Maigret was still in his office, in his shirt-sleeves, for the room was over-heated and the air blue with tobacco-smoke.

'Sit down. Tell me everything.'

Janvier recounted what he had done and what he had discovered.

'I have ordered the stations to be watched,' the inspector said, when Janvier had finished. 'Up to now, Pierrot has not tried to catch a train.'

He showed him an identification card on which there were full-face and profile photographs of a man who did not look thirty, but much younger.

'Is that Pierrot?'

'Yes. He was first arrested when he was twenty for assault and battery during a brawl in a bar in the Rue de Flandre. The second time, a year and a half later, he was suspected of being an accomplice in the robbery of a client, committed by a prostitute with whom he was living, but nothing was proved. He was last arrested when he was twenty-four for living on immoral earnings. At that time he had no job and was dependent on a girl named Ernestine. Since then, there has been nothing against him. I have circulated his description to all police stations. Is Janin still watching the hotel?'

'Yes, I thought it wise.'

'Well done. I don't think he will go back there for some time to come, but we mustn't take risks. On the other hand, I need Janin. I am going to send young Lapointe to relieve him. You see, I should be surprised if Pierrot did try to leave Paris. He has spent his entire life in a district he knows like the back of his hand, and it is easy for him to vanish in it. Janin is more at home in that district than we are. Get Lapointe.'

Lapointe listened to his instructions and rushed out into the street as eagerly as if the whole investigation rested with him.

'I have also looked up Louise Filon's file.

'Between the ages of fifteen and twenty-four she was picked up more than a hundred times by the Black Maria, taken to the station, examined, placed under observation and for the most part released again within a few days.

'That's all,' Maigret said with a sigh, knocking out his pipe on his heel. 'Or rather it is not quite all, but the rest is more indefinite.'

Perhaps he was really talking to himself, to sort out his ideas, but Janvier was none the less flattered at being taken into his confidence.

'Somewhere there lives the man who set Lulu up in the Avenue Carnot flat. First thing this morning, it bothered me to find a girl like her living in that house. You know what I mean?'

'Yes.'

It was not the kind of block of flats in which kept women are usually found. It was not even the right district. The house in the Avenue Carnot smelt of the respectable, well-to-do middle-classes, and it was surprising that the proprietor or manager should have accepted a prostitute as a tenant.

'It first occurred to me that if her lover installed her there, it was to keep her near his own home. Now the fact is that, if the concierge is telling the truth, Lulu received no callers except for Pierrot. Nor did she go out regularly, and it sometimes happened that she stayed at home for a whole week on end.'

'I think I understand.'

'Understand what?'

Janvier confessed with a blush:

'I don't know.'

'Nor do I. I am only making assumptions. The man's slippers and dressing-gown found in the cupboard certainly did not belong to the saxophonist. At the shirt-makers in the Rue de Rivoli they cannot say who bought the dressing-gown. They have hundreds of customers and don't record the names of cash customers. As for the shoe-maker, he's a real character who claims that he has no time to examine his books at present, but promises to do so one of these days. The fact remains that some man other than Pierrot used to call on her, and was sufficiently intimate with her to wear his dressing-gown and slippers. If the concierge never caught sight of him . . .'

'Then he must have lived in the same block?'

'That's the logical explanation.'

'Have you a list of the tenants?'

'Lucas has just let me have it by telephone.'

Janvier wondered why his chief had assumed his cross-tempered look, as if something in this case displeased him.

'What you have told me about Lulu's illness and her operation might provide a clue, and in that event . . .'

He paused to light his pipe, and bent over the list of names on his desk.

'Do you know who lives immediately above her flat? Professor Gouin, the surgeon, who, as it happens, is the greatest specialist in brain operations.'

Janvier's reaction was to ask:

'Is he married?'

'Yes, he's married, and his wife lives with him.'

'What are you going to do?'

'First, have a talk with the concierge. Even if she did tell me the truth this morning, she certainly didn't tell me the whole truth. Perhaps I shall also go to see Madame Brault, who's probably in the same boat.'

'What do you want me to do?'

'Stay here. When Janin telephones, ask him to start a search for Pierrot in his district. Send a photograph over to him.'

It was five o'clock, and night was falling as

Maigret crossed town in a police car. That morning, when his wife was looking out of the window to see how people were dressed, an odd idea had crossed his mind. It had occurred to him that the day exactly fulfilled his general conception of what a 'working day' should be like. Those two words had entered his head quite irrationally, as one suddenly recalls the refrain of a song. It was a day on which it was unthinkable that people should go out of doors for pleasure, or that they should find any place at all in which to enjoy themselves; it was a day in which to be busy, to do grimly what had to be done, splashing through the rain into Metro stations, shops and offices, surrounded by damp monotonous greyness.

So had passed his own working day; his office was as warm as an oven, and he could work up little interest in the event when he once more arrived in the Avenue Carnot, where the huge stone block of flats seemed totally devoid of attraction. That fine fellow, Lucas, was still there, in the third-floor flat, and Maigret observed him from below, parting the curtains and gazing gloomily into the street.

Sitting in front of the round table in the lodge, the concierge was busily mending sheets. Wearing her spectacles, she looked older. It was warm in here too, and peaceful, with an old clock ticking, and the gas-stove in the kitchen hissing.

'Don't worry. I've just come in to have a little chat.'

'Are you sure that she was murdered?' she

asked as he was taking off his overcoat and sitting down, familiarly, facing her.

'Unless someone removed the gun after she died, which seems unlikely. The charwoman was only a few minutes alone up there, and before she left I made sure that she was taking nothing away with her. Of course, I did not put her through a thorough search. What are you thinking about, Madame Cornet?'

'Nothing in particular. Just about that poor girl.'

'You're sure you told me this morning everything you know?'

He saw her blush, and bend her head over her needle-work. A few moments went by before she said:

'Why do you ask me that?'

'Because I have an idea that you know the man who set up Louise Filon in this house. Was it you who let him the flat?'

'No. It was the manager.'

'I shall go and see him; no doubt he'll be better informed. I think I shall also go up to the fourth floor where I have some inquiries to make.'

At this she quickly looked up.

'To the fourth floor?'

'That's Professor Gouin's flat, isn't it? I understand his wife and he occupy the whole floor.'

'Yes.'

She had recovered her composure. He went on:

'In any case, I can ask them if they heard anything yesterday evening. Were they in?'

'Madame Gouin was.'

'All day?'

'Yes. Her sister came to see her and stayed till eleven-thirty.'

'And the Professor?'

'He left for the hospital at eight o'clock.'

'When did he return?'

'About eleven-fifteen. A little after that, his sister-in-law left.'

'Does the Professor often visit the hospital at night?'

'Not very often. Only when there is an emergency case.'

'Is he upstairs at present?'

'No. He hardly ever comes home before dinner-time. He has an office in his flat, but he doesn't receive patients here save in exceptional circumstances.'

'I shall go and speak to his wife.'

She watched him rise and walk to the chair on which he had placed his overcoat. He was about to open the door when she murmured:

'Monsieur Maigret!'

He had been rather expecting this, and turned round, smiling slightly. While she was groping for words, with an almost pleading expression, he observed:

'So he's the one?'

She misunderstood him.

'You don't mean to say it was the Professor who . . . ?'

'Certainly not. That's not what I meant. What

I am almost sure about is that the Professor introduced Louise Filon into this house.'

Reluctantly she nodded.

'Why didn't you tell me?'

'You did not ask me.'

'I asked you if you knew the man who . . .'

'No. You asked me whether I sometimes saw
anyone else go up to the flat besides the musician.'

Discussion was useless.

'Has the Professor asked you to keep mum?'

'No. It doesn't matter to him.'

'How do you know?'

'Because he is never secretive.'

'Then why didn't you tell me? . . .'

'I don't know. I didn't think there was any
point in implicating him. He saved my son's life.
He operated on him free of charge, and treated
him for over two years.'

'Where is your son?'

'In the army. In Indo-China.'

'Does Madame Gouin know the truth?'

'Yes. She's not jealous; she's used to it.'

'In short, the whole house knew that Lulu was
the Professor's mistress?'

'If they didn't know, it was because they didn't
care to. The tenants here don't bother about one
another's affairs. He often went down to the
third floor wearing pyjamas and a dressing-
gown.'

'What sort of a man is he?'

'Don't you know him?'

She looked at Maigret with a disappointed air. The inspector had often seen Gouin's picture in the papers but had never had occasion to meet him personally.

'He must be nearly sixty, isn't he?'

'Sixty-two. He doesn't look it. Besides for men like him, age doesn't matter.'

Maigret dimly remembered a powerful head, with a strong nose and determined chin, but with cheeks a little sunken and bags under the eyes. It was amusing to see the concierge speaking of him as enthusiastically as a young girl might about her piano-teacher.

'You don't know whether he saw her yesterday before he left for the hospital?'

'I told you that it was only eight o'clock, and the young man came in later.'

All that interested her was to keep Gouin out of it.

'But after he returned?'

She was obviously groping for the best reply.

'Certainly not.'

'Why?'

'Because his sister-in-law came down some minutes after he went up.'

'You think that he met his sister-in-law?'

'I expect she was waiting for him to arrive before she left.'

'You're warmly defending him, Madame Cornet.'

'I am only telling the truth.'

'As Madame Gouin is in the know, there's no reason why I shouldn't go to see her.'

'Do you think that's tactful?'

'Perhaps not. You're right.'

Nevertheless, he started for the door.

'Where are you going?'

'Upstairs. I shall leave the door half-open, and when the Professor comes in I shall ask him for a moment's interview.'

'I suppose you must.'

'Thank you.'

He thought her likeable. Now the door was shut, he turned round to look at her through the glass. She had risen, and seeing him, seemed to regret having moved so quickly. She entered the kitchen as if she had something urgent to do, but he was convinced it was not to the kitchen she had meant to run; much more likely, it was to the table near the window where the telephone stood.

3

'WHERE did you find it?' Maigret asked Lucas.

'On the top shelf in the kitchen cupboard.'

It was a white cardboard shoe-box, and Lucas had left on the table the red string with which it had been tied when he found it. Its contents reminded Maigret of other 'treasures' that he had so often come across in the country or among poor people—the marriage lines, a few yellowing letters, perhaps a pawnbroker's receipt—not always kept in a box, but sometimes in the best soup-tureen or fruit-dish.

Louise Filon's treasures were not so very different from these. They contained no marriage lines, but a birth certificate issued at the town hall in the XVIIIth *arrondissement*, stating that the said Louise Marie Josephine Filon was born in Paris, the daughter of a certain Louis Filon, tripe-seller, resident in the Rue de Cambrai, near the slaughter-houses of La Vilette, and of Philippine Le Flem, washerwoman.

The photograph, taken by a local photographer, was probably of the mother. The traditional backcloth displayed a park with a balustrade in the foreground. The woman, who must have been about thirty when the picture was taken, had not managed to summon up a smile at the photographer's command, and she stared straight ahead. She must have borne several other children besides Louise, for her figure was gross and her breasts hung flabbily in her bodice.

Lucas had seated himself in the armchair he had been occupying before opening the door for the inspector. The latter could not help smiling when he came in, for lying open, near the cigarette burning in an ash-tray, was one of Lulu's pot-boilers which the sergeant must have picked up out of boredom, and nearly half of which he had read.

'She died,' Lucas said, pointing to the photograph, 'seven years ago.'

He handed his chief an old newspaper cutting from the births, deaths and marriages column, listing the persons deceased on that day; among them was the name of Philippine Filon, née Le Flem.

The two men had left the door half-open, and Maigret had an ear cocked for the sound of the lift. The only time that it had been used, it had stopped at the second floor.

'What about her father?'

'Only this letter.'

It was written in pencil on cheap paper, and the handwriting was of someone who had not had much schooling.

'*My dear Louise,*

This is just to say that I am in hospital again and in a very bad way. Perhaps you will be kind enough to send me a little tobacco money. They say that it is not good for me to eat and they are letting me die of hunger. I am sending this letter to a bar where someone here says he saw you. I expect they will know you there. I shan't make old bones.

Father.

At the top was the name of a hospital at Béziers in Hérault. As there was no date, it was impossible to tell when the letter had been written, though to judge by the yellowing paper, it must have been two or three years ago.

Had Louise Filon received any other letters? Why had she kept only this one? Was it because her father had died shortly afterwards?

'You can find out from Béziers.'

'Very good, Chief.'

Maigret discovered no more letters, only photographs, most of them taken at fairs, some showing Louise alone, and others accompanied by Pierrot. There were also identity pictures of the girl, taken by automatic machines.

The rest consisted of small odds and ends, won at the fair—a china dog, an ash-tray, an elephant in spun glass, and even some paper flowers.

It would have been quite natural to have unearthed such petty treasures in the Barbès district or around the Boulevard de la Chapelle. Here in an Avenue Carnot flat the cardboard box became almost tragic.

'Nothing else?'

As Lucas was about to reply, they were startled by the ringing of the telephone. Maigret quickly lifted the receiver.

'Hello!' he said.

'Is Monsieur Maigret there?' said a woman's voice.

'Speaking.'

'I am sorry to trouble you, Inspector. I spoke to your office and they told me that you were probably here or on your way. This is Madame Gouin speaking.'

'Yes, madame.'

'May I come down and have a talk with you?'

'Wouldn't it be easier if I came up to you?'

The voice was firm. It continued so as she replied:

'I'd rather come down, so that my husband won't find you in our flat when he returns.'

'As you wish.'

'I'll come at once.'

Maigret had time to breathe a word to Lucas:

'It's Professor Gouin's wife, who lives on the next floor.'

A few seconds later they heard steps on the staircase, then someone passed through the front door, which was open, and shut it. There was a knock on the half-open vestibule door and Maigret stepped forward, saying:

'Come in, madame.'

She did so with poise, as she might have entered any other flat, and, without looking round the room, fixed her eyes at once on Maigret.

'May I introduce Sergeant Lucas. If you would like to sit down?'

'Thank you.'

She was tall and well-made, without being stout. If Gouin was sixty-two, she was probably forty-five, and scarcely looked it.

'I suppose you were rather expecting me to call,' she said with the hint of a smile.

'The concierge warned you?'

She hesitated a moment, her eyes on his, and her smile became more pronounced.

'Yes, she did. She has just telephoned me.'

'Then you knew I was here. If you telephoned my office, it was merely to make your actions seem spontaneous.'

She blushed faintly, and lost none of her self-possession.

'I should have suspected that you'd guess. But, believe me, I would have got into touch with you anyway. Ever since this morning, when I heard what had happened here, I've been meaning to talk to you.'

'Why didn't you do so?'

'Perhaps because I'd have preferred my husband to be kept out of this business.'

Maigret had not ceased observing her. He noted that she had not spared a glance for their surroundings, nor shown any sign of curiosity.

'When were you last in this flat, madame?'

Once more there was a slight blush on her cheeks, but she parried gamely.

'Ah! so you know that too? Yet nobody could have told you. Not even Madame Cornet.'

She thought for a moment, but did not take long to find an answer to the riddle.

'I probably didn't behave like someone entering a flat for the first time, especially a flat that has been the scene of a murder.'

Lucas was now sitting on the sofa, almost on the spot occupied that morning by Louise Filon's corpse. Madame Gouin had settled into an armchair, and Maigret was standing, his back to the fireplace, which was filled with sham logs.

'In any case, I will tell you. One night, seven or eight months ago, the person who lived here called me, in a state of panic, because my husband had just suffered a heart attack.'

'Was he in the bedroom?'

'Yes, I came down and gave him first aid.'

'You've studied medicine?'

'Before we married I was a nurse.'

Ever since she had appeared, Maigret had been wondering what class she belonged to, without being able to find the answer. Now he had a better understanding of her kind of self-possession.

'Go on.'

'That's almost all. I was going to telephone one of our doctor friends, when Etienne came to and forbade me to call anyone.'

'Was he surprised to find you at his bedside?'

'No. He always kept me informed. He never kept anything from me. That night he came upstairs with me and finally went peacefully to sleep.'

'Was that his first attack?'

'He had had a milder one three years earlier.'

She was composed and self-possessed, as if she were still in nurse's uniform and at a patient's bedside. Lucas was the one who was astonished; he was not up to date on the situation, and did not understand how a wife could speak so calmly about her husband's mistress.

'Why,' Maigret asked, 'did you want to talk to me tonight?'

'The concierge told me that you intend to question my husband. I wondered whether this could be avoided, and whether you might not get the information you want by interviewing me. Do you know the Professor?'

'Only by repute.'

'He is an outstanding man; there are only one or two like him in each generation.'

The inspector nodded in agreement.

'He dedicates his whole life to his work which is a real mission for him. Besides his lectures and consultations at the Cochin Hospital, it often happens that he performs three or four operations a day, and, as I expect you know, they are extremely delicate operations. You can't be surprised that I do my utmost to spare him any worry.'

'Have you seen your husband since Louise Filon's death?'

'He came in to lunch. This morning, when he left, there was already some activity in the flat, but we knew nothing then.'

'What was his attitude at lunch?'

'It has been a blow for him.'

'He was in love with her?'

She looked at him for an instant without replying. Then she glanced at Lucas whose presence she seemed to find irksome.

'From what I have heard of you, Monsieur Maigret, I think you are a man of understanding. It is precisely because other people wouldn't understand that I wanted to prevent the news of this affair from spreading. The Professor is a man who ought not to be subject to ill-natured gossip, and his work is too precious for everybody to run the risk of reducing its value by causing him unnecessary worry.'

In spite of himself, the inspector glanced at the spot where Lulu's corpse had lain that morning, as if in commentary on the words 'unnecessary worry.'

'May I try to give you a sketch of his character?'

'Please do.'

'You probably know that he was born into a poor peasant family in the Cevennes?'

'I knew he came from peasant stock.'

'What he has achieved, he has done by sheer

will-power. It might be said, almost without ex-
aggerating, that he never had a childhood, nor
a youth. You follow what I mean?'

'Indeed I do.'

'He is a kind of force of nature. Although I
am his wife, I may add that he is a man of genius,
for other people have said so before me, and
they will go on saying so.'

Maigret again agreed.

'People in general have a curious attitude towards geniuses. They are quite prepared to admit that they are different from others where
intelligence and professional activity are concerned. Any patient will think it normal that
Gouin should get up at two in the morning to
perform an urgent operation which he alone can
carry out, and at nine o'clock be in the hospital
attending to his other cases. Yet these same patients would be shocked to learn that in other
ways, too, he is different from them.'

Maigret could guess what was to follow, but
he preferred to let her talk. Besides, she was
doing so with a convincing calmness.

'Etienne has never bothered with the minor
pleasures of life. He has, as it were, no friends.
I do not remember him taking a real holiday.
The energy he uses up is unbelievable. And the
only way in which he has ever been able to relax
is with women.'

She glanced at Lucas, and turned back to Maigret.

'I hope I haven't shocked you?'

'Not at all.'

'You do know what I mean? He isn't a man who would pay court to women. He hasn't the patience, nor the inclination. What he wants from them is a brutal release, and I do not think he has ever been really in love in his life.'

'Not even with you?'

'I've often wondered. I don't know. We have been married now for twenty-two years. At that time, he was a bachelor living with an old house-keeper.'

'In this house?'

'Yes. He took the lease of our flat by chance when he was thirty and he has never thought of moving since, even when he was appointed to Cochin which is at the other end of the town.'

'Did you work for him?'

'Yes. I suppose I can speak freely.'

The presence of Lucas was still embarrassing her, and Lucas, who knew it, was ill at ease, crossing and uncrossing his short legs.

'For months he paid no attention to me. Like everyone in the hospital, I knew that most of the nurses went through it some day or other, and that it was of no consequence. The next day he didn't even seem to remember. One night when I was on duty, and we had to wait for the result of a three-hour operation, he took me, without a word.'

'Were you in love with him?'

'I think I was. In any case, I admired him. A few days later I was astonished when he invited me to lunch in a restaurant in the Faubourg Saint-Jacques. He asked me whether I was married.

55

Up to then he hadn't troubled about it. He inquired who my parents were and I told him my father was a fisherman in Brittany. Am I boring you?'

'Not at all.'

'I so much want you to understand him.'

'Are you afraid that he'll come home and be surprised not to find you?'

'Before I came down, I spoke to the Saint-Joseph Clinic, where he is operating at the moment, and I know he won't be back before half past seven.'

It was a quarter past six.

'What was I saying? Oh yes. We were lunching together and he wanted to know what my father did. Now, things get more difficult. Especially since I shouldn't like you to misunderstand. What most people don't know is that he is terribly timid, I might say morbidly timid, but only in relation to people belonging to a different social class. I suppose it was because of this that at the age of forty he was still unmarried and had never moved in what is called society. All the girls he took came from the lower classes.'

'I see.'

'With any other kind of girl I wonder whether he could have . . .'

She blushed at the words, giving them a precise meaning.

'He got used to me, while still carrying on with the others as he always had done. Then one fine day, almost absent-mindedly, he asked me to marry him. That's the whole of our story. I came to live here. I kept house for him.'

'The housekeeper left?'

'A week after our wedding. There's no need to add that I am not jealous. That would be absurd on my part.'

Maigret could not recall ever having studied someone quite so intently as he was studying this woman; she knew it, and was not intimidated; on the contrary she appeared to understand the kind of interest he was taking in her.

She was trying to tell him everything, leaving no trait of her great man's character unilluminated.

'He has gone on sleeping with the nurses, with his successive assistants, and, in fact, with every girl who comes to hand and who is not likely to complicate his life. Perhaps that is the main point. Nothing in the world would induce him to start an affair that might lose him time that he considers sacred to his work.'

'Lulu?'

'You already know she was called Lulu? I'm coming to that. You'll see that it's just as simple as the rest of it. May I fetch a glass of water?'

Lucas was about to get up, but she had already passed through the kitchen door and they could hear the tap running. When she sat down again, her lips were damp and a drop of water clung to her chin.

She was not pretty in the ordinary sense of the word, nor beautiful, in spite of her regular features. But she was attractive to look at. There was a sort of soothing influence about her. As a patient, Maigret would have enjoyed being nursed by her. She was also the kind of woman with whom one could go out lunching or dining without troubling to keep the conversation going. A girl friend, in fact, who would understand everything, and never be surprised nor shocked nor angry.

'I suppose you know how old he is?'

'Sixty-two.'

'Yes. Mind you he has lost none of his vigour. And I use the word in its fullest sense. I think, however, that all men of a certain age are terrified by the idea of losing their virility.'

While she was speaking she recollected that Maigret himself was over fifty, and suddenly stammered:

'I beg your pardon.'

'Not at all.'

For the first time they smiled at each other.

'I suppose it is the same with other men. I don't know. But the fact is that Etienne put more furious energy than ever into his sexual activities. I hope I'm not shocking you?'

'By no means.'

'About two years ago, he had a young patient, Louise Filon, whose life he quite miraculously saved. I suppose you already know what her life had been? She came from as near the gutter as anyone can, and that is probably what interested my husband.'

Maigret nodded agreement, for everything she

said sounded true, and had the simplicity of a police report.

'It must have started at the hospital, when she was convalescent. Later, he set her up in a flat in the Rue La Fayette, after mentioning it to me incidentally. He never went into details. He was very reserved about such things, and still is. Unexpectedly over a meal he'd tell me what he had done or what he meant to do. I never asked him questions. And then we never spoke of it again.'

'Was it you who suggested that she should come and live in this block?'

She seemed pleased that Maigret should have guessed.

'To help you grasp it, I must give you a few more details. I apologize for taking so long. But it all hangs together. At one time Etienne used to drive his own car. Then, some years ago, four to be exact, he had a slight accident in the Place de la Concorde. He knocked down a woman, passing by, who luckily suffered nothing more than contusions. Nevertheless, he was much upset. For some months we had a chauffeur, but Etienne could never get used to it. It shocked him that a man in the prime of his life should have nothing to do but wait for him by the kerb for hours at a time. I suggested that I should drive, but that wasn't practical either, and he fell into the habit of taking taxis. The car stayed in the garage for several months and in the end we sold it.

'It is always the same taxi that comes to fetch

59

him in the morning and does a part of his rounds with him. It is some way from here to the Faubourg Saint-Jacques. He also has patients at Neuilly, and often in the other city hospitals. To have to go to the Rue La Fayette in addition . . .'

Maigret was still nodding assent, while Lucas seemed to be dozing.

'Quite by chance, a flat fell vacant in this house.'

'One moment. Did your husband often stay the night at the Rue La Fayette?'

'Only part of the night. He insisted on being here in the morning when his assistant who acts as his secretary arrives.'

She gave a little laugh.

'In a way domestic complications brought about everything. I asked why he didn't set the girl up here.'

'You knew who she was?'

'I knew all about her, including the fact that she had a lover named Pierrot.'

'Your husband knew, too?'

'Yes. He wasn't jealous. Probably he wouldn't have liked to find him with Lulu, but so long as things happened without his knowing . . .'

'Go on. He accepted your proposal. What about her?'

'It seems that she held off for a while.'

'What in your opinion were Louise Filon's feelings for the Professor?'

Maigret was automatically beginning to speak in the same tones as Madame Gouin about this man whom he had never seen, but who seemed to be almost present in the room.

60

'Shall I be frank?'

'Please do.'

'In the first place, like all women who meet him, she fell under his influence. You may be thinking that this is a curious kind of pride on my part, but though he isn't what might be called handsome, and he's far from young, I knew few women who have resisted him. Instinctively, women feel his strength and . . .'

This time she could not find the words that she wanted.

'At any rate, it's a fact, and I don't think that anyone you question will deny it. It was the same with this girl as with the others. Furthermore, he had saved her life and had treated her in a way she wasn't used to being treated.'

It was all straightforward and logical.

'I am convinced, to be completely frank, that the question of money played its part. If not the money itself, at least the prospect of a certain security, of a life free from worry.'

'Did she ever speak of leaving him to follow her lover?'

'Not to my knowledge.'

'Have you ever seen this man?'

'I have passed him in the entrance-hall.'

'Did he come often?'

'In general, no. She used to meet him in the afternoons, I don't know where. But on occasion it happened that he came to see her.'

'Did your husband know?'

'He may have.'

'Would it have annoyed him?'

'Possibly, though not because of jealousy. It is hard to explain.'

'Was your husband greatly attached to this girl?'

'She owed him everything. He had practically created her, since without him she would have been dead. Perhaps he was thinking of the day when there would be no more girls for him? Then again, though this is only an assumption, with her he was ashamed of nothing.'

'And with you?'

For a moment she glanced away at the carpet.

'After all, I am a woman.'

He almost retorted:

'Whereas she was nothing!'

For that was indeed the thought she had in mind, and perhaps the Professor shared it?

He decided to say nothing. All three of them remained silent for a moment. The rain outside was still falling noiselessly. In the house opposite the windows were lit up, and a shadow moved behind the cream curtains in one of the flats.

'Tell me about yesterday evening,' Maigret eventually suggested, adding, as he held out his pipe which he had just filled:

'May I?'

'Please do.'

Up till then he had been so interested in Madame Gouin that he had not thought about smoking.

'What would you like me to tell you?'

'To begin with, a detail. Was your husband in the habit of spending the night with her?'

'Very rarely. Up above we occupy the whole floor. On the left is what we call the flat. On the right, my husband has a bedroom and bathroom, a library, another where he stacks scientific publications, on every square inch of space, finally his office and his secretary's office.'

'You sleep in separate bedrooms?'

'We always have. Our rooms are separated only by a dressing-room.'

'May I ask you an indiscreet question?'

'You are fully entitled to do so.'

'Do you still have marital relations with your husband?'

She glanced once more at poor Lucas who felt he was one too many, and did not know what to do with himself.

'Seldom.'

'You mean practically never?'

'Yes.'

'Since when?'

'For years.'

'You don't miss it?'

She was not startled, smiled, and shook her head.

'It is a confession you're asking of me, and I am ready to answer as frankly as I can. Let us say that I do miss it a bit.'

'You don't let him see that?'

'Certainly not.'

'Have you a lover?'

'The idea has never occurred to me.'

She paused, her eyes on his.

'You do believe me?'

'Yes.'

'Thank you. People don't always accept the truth. When one lives with a man like Gouin, one is prepared to make some sacrifices.'

'He used to come down to her and then go up again?'

'Yes.'

'Did he do so yesterday?'

'No. It didn't happen every day. Sometimes a few minutes' visit satisfied him for nearly a week. It depended on his work. Probably it depended, too, on what opportunities he found elsewhere.'

'He didn't stop having relations with other women?'

'The kind of relations I have described.'

'And yesterday . . . ?'

'He saw her for a few minutes after dinner. I know because he didn't take the lift when he left, which is a sure sign.'

'How can you be certain that he only stayed a few minutes?'

'Because I heard him come out of this flat and ring for the lift.'

'You were spying on him?'

'You are a terror, Monsieur Maigret. Yes, I was spying on him, as I always do, not because of jealousy, but . . . How shall I explain without seeming conceited? Because I consider it my duty to protect him, to know everything he does, where he is, and to follow him in my thoughts.'

'What time was it?'

'About eight o'clock. We had eaten dinner quickly, because he had to spend the evening at Cochin. He was anxious about the results of an operation he had performed that afternoon and he wanted to be within reach of the patient.'

'So he spent some minutes in this flat and then took the lift?'

'Yes. His assistant, Mademoiselle Decaux, was waiting for him downstairs, as she does when he is returning at night to the hospital. She lives round the corner, in the Rue des Acacias, and they always make the journey together.'

'She, too?' he asked, giving an obvious meaning to the words.

'She, too, occasionally. Does it seem preposterous to you?'

'No.'

'Where was I? My sister arrived at half past eight.'

'Does she live in Paris?'

'In the Boulevard Saint-Michel, opposite the School of Mining. Antoinette is five years older than I am and has never married. She works in a municipal library and is a typical old maid.'

'Does she know about the life your husband leads?'

'She doesn't know everything. But from what she has found out, she hates him and despises him deeply.'

65

'They do not get on?'

'She never exchanges a word with him. My sister is still a great Catholic, and for her Gouin is the devil himself.'

'And how does he treat her?'

'He ignores her. She seldom calls here, and then only when I'm alone in the house.'

'She avoids him?'

'As often as she can.'

'Yesterday, however . . .'

'I see that the concierge has told you everything. It is true that yesterday they did meet. I wasn't expecting my husband before midnight at the earliest. And my sister and I were chatting.'

'About what?'

'Nothing in particular.'

'Did you discuss Lulu?'

'I don't think so.'

'But you're not sure?'

'In fact, I am. I don't know why I answered evasively. We talked about our parents.'

'Are they dead?'

'My mother is dead, but my father is still alive in Finistère. We have some other sisters down there, too. We were six girls and two boys.'

'Do any of them live in Paris?'

'Only Antoinette and I. At half past eleven, or a little earlier, we were surprised to hear the door opening and to see Etienne coming in. All he did was nod. Antoinette said good-bye and left almost immediately.'

'Your husband did not go downstairs?'

'No. He was tired and anxious about his patient whose condition was not so satisfactory as he would have wished.'

'I suppose he had a key to this flat?'

'Of course.'

'During the evening, did anything unusual happen? Did you or your sister hear any noises?'

'In these old stone houses you can hear nothing between one flat and another, still less between one floor and another.'

She looked at her wrist-watch and showed signs of impatience.

'Forgive me, but it's time I went upstairs. Etienne may be coming in at any minute. Have you any further questions?'

'None at the moment.'

'Do you think you will be able to avoid questioning him?'

'It is impossible to make any promise, but I shall only trouble your husband if I consider it essential.'

'What do you feel about it at present?'

'At present I do not think it essential.'

She rose and held out her hand, as a man might have done, still looking him in the eye.

'Thank you, Monsieur Maigret.'

As she turned, her glance fell on the cardboard box and on the photographs, but the inspector could not see the expression on her face.

'I am at home all day. You may come when my husband is out. And I mention that, of course, not as an order but as an entreaty.'

'I gathered that instantly.'

She repeated:

'Thank you.'

So she went out, shutting the two doors behind her, while little Lucas looked at the inspector with the air of a man who has just been hit on the head. He was so afraid of saying something stupid that he remained silent, watching Maigret's face in the hope of being able to read on it what he should think.

4

ODDLY enough, in the car taking him back to the P.J. Maigret was thinking not about Professor Gouin, nor his wife, but, almost half-consciously, about Louise Filon. Before leaving he had slipped into his wallet the photographs of her taken at the fair.

Even though these pictures had been taken on evenings when she should have been enjoying herself, there was no happiness in her face. Maigret had known many girls like her, born in the same surroundings and who had experienced more or less the same kind of childhood and life. Some of them had possessed a crude noisy cheerfulness that could at a moment's notice give way to tears or rebellion. Others, like Désirée Brault, especially as they grew older, became hard and cynical.

It was difficult to define the expression he observed in Lulu's pictures, and which she must have worn all through her life. It was not a question of melancholy, but rather the sulky look of a little girl who stands apart in the school-yard watching her companions at play.

He would have been hard put to it to explain why she had been attractive, but he sensed it, and it had often happened, in spite of himself, that he had been more gentle than with others, in questioning girls like this.

They were young and still gifted with a certain bloom; in some respects, they seemed hardly to have emerged from childhood, and yet they had lived through much and there were already too many loathsome memories in their eyes, which no longer sparkled, and their bodies had the unhealthy charm of a thing about to wither, or half withered already.

He pictured her in the hotel room in the Rue Riquet, or in any other room in the Barbès district, spending her days reading on the bed, sleeping, or gazing out of the greenish windows. He pictured her sitting for hours in one of the cafés of the XVIIIth *arrondissement*, while Pierrot and three friends played *belote*. He could see her also, serious-looking and almost transfigured, dancing in a cheap dive. And he pictured her, planted on a street corner watching for the lurking shadows of men, never taking the trouble to smile, and, later, climbing up the stairs of a lodging-house ahead of them, calling out her name to the landlady.

For more than a year she had lived in the imposing stone block in the Avenue Carnot, in a flat that seemed too big and chill for her; and that was where he had difficulty in picturing her; in front of a man like Etienne Gouin.

Most of the lights at the Quai des Orfèvres had been switched off. Slowly he climbed the stairs, still soiled with the footprints of damp soles, and opened his office door. Janvier was waiting for him. It was the time of year when the contrast is most marked between the cold outside and the warmth of buildings, which seem so overheated that at first entry the blood rushes to the head.

'Anything new?'

The whole machinery of the police was busy with Pierre Eyraud. In the railway stations, inspectors were stopping travellers whose descriptions tallied with his. And at the airfields, too. The lodging-house squad would also be on the job, sifting through the hotels and furnished rooms of the XVIIIth *arrondissement*.

Ever since early afternoon, young Lapointe had been kicking his heels in the Rue Riquet outside the Hotel du Var, around which, now that night had fallen, the girls were on the prowl.

As for Inspector Janin, the local man, he was devoting himself to more specialized inquiries. . . . That north-east corner of Paris is a real jungle of stone, in which a man could disappear for months, and where often a crime never comes to light until months after it has been committed; thousands of people, men and women, live on the edge of the law in a world where they find as many hiding places and accomplices as they can wish; and where, from time to time, the police throw out a dragnet, and by accident they fish up someone for whom they are looking, but they rely much more upon a telephone call from a jealous prostitute or an informer.

'Gastine-Renette called an hour ago.'

The ballistics expert.

'What did he say?'

'You will have his written report tomorrow morning. The bullet that killed Louise Filon was fired from a .25 automatic.'

At the P.J. they called it an amateur's weapon. Hoodlums, who really intend to kill, use more impressive guns.

'Dr. Paul also called. He asks you to get in touch with him.'

Janvier looked at the clock. It was a little after seven-fifteen.

'He should have arrived at the restaurant La Pérouse where he is taking the chair at a dinner.'

Maigret called the restaurant. A few minutes later he had the medical examiner on the line.

'I have carried out the autopsy on the girl you sent me. If I'm not mistaken, I think I have seen her before.'

'She's been under arrest several times.'

The doctor had certainly not recognized Lulu's face, disfigured as it was by the revolver shot, but her body.

'Of course the shot was fired point-blank. One does not need to be an expert to perceive that.

I reckon the distance to have been between twelve and fifteen inches, not more.'

'I suppose death was instantaneous?'

'Absolutely instantaneous. The stomach still contained undigested food, lobster among other things.'

Maigret recalled seeing in the kitchen garbage-pail an empty lobster tin.

'She drank white wine with her meal. Are you interested in that?'

Maigret did not know. At this stage of the investigation, it was impossible to tell what might become important.

'I discovered something else which may surprise you. Did you know the girl was pregnant?'

Maigret was indeed surprised, so much so that he was silent for a moment.

'How many months?' he eventually asked.

'About six weeks. Very likely she didn't know it. If she did, it can't have been for long.'

'I suppose this is definite?'

'Absolutely. You will see the technical details in my report.'

Maigret hung up, and said to Janvier who was standing waiting in the office:

'She was pregnant.'

But Janvier, who knew only the broad outlines of the case, remained unmoved.

'What shall we do with Lapointe?'

'Quite so. We must send someone to relieve him.'

'There is Lober, who is doing nothing in particular.'

'We must also relieve Lucas. It probably won't serve any purpose, but I should prefer to go on having the flat guarded.'

'If I can take time for a bite, I'll go myself. Would it be in order to sleep on the job?'

'I see no reason against it.'

Maigret glanced through the latest editions of the newspapers. There was still no picture of Pierrot. Presumably it had arrived too late for the news-editors, but they had published a full description:

The police are searching for the lover of the Filon girl, a musician in a dance-band, named Pierre Eyraud, known as Pierrot. He was her last caller yesterday evening. . . .

'Pierre Eyraud, who has had several convictions, has disappeared, and it is presumed that he is hiding in the La Chapelle district which he knows well.'

Maigret shrugged his shoulders, rose, and paused before going to the door.

'If there is anything new, shall I call you at home?'

He said yes. There was no reason to stay in the office. He was driven back home in one of the cars and, as usual, Madame Maigret opened the door of the flat before he had turned the knob. She did not tell him that he was late. Dinner was ready.

'You didn't catch cold?'

'I don't think so.'

'You ought to change your shoes.'

'My feet aren't wet.'

74

Which was true, for he had not done any walking during the day. He saw on a chair the same newspaper he had been looking at in the P.J. His wife must know about the case, but she asked no questions.

She knew that he meant to go out again, for he had not taken off his tie as he nearly always did. Dinner over, she followed him with her eyes as he opened the sideboard cupboard to pour himself a glass of *prunelle*.

'You're going out?'

A moment earlier, he had not been sure. In fact, he had been half expecting Professor Gouin to telephone him. This was not founded on anything definite. But would it not occur to Gouin that the police would like to question him? Surely he would be surprised at not being approached, when so many people knew about his relations with Louise Filon.

He called Louise Filon's flat. Janvier had just settled in.

'Anything new?'

'Nothing, Chief. I have warned my wife. I am quite happy. I shall spend the night on this wonderful sofa.'

'Do you know if the Professor has returned?'

'Lucas told me he went up at seven-thirty. I haven't heard him go out.'

'Good night.'

Had Gouin guessed that his wife would speak to Maigret? Was she capable of not letting on? What had they talked about between themselves while they were dining alone together? When dinner was over did the Professor generally withdraw into his office?

Maigret helped himself to a second glass which he drank standing next to the sideboard, then he went to the coat-rack and took down his heavy overcoat.

'Better take a scarf. Do you expect to be out long?'

'An hour or two.'

He had to walk as far as the Boulevard Voltaire before finding a taxi, to which he gave the address of the Grelot. There was not much life in the streets, except round the Gare de l'Est and the Gare du Nord, and the latter always reminded Maigret of his early years in the police force.

In the Boulevard de la Chapelle, beneath the elevated Metro, the familiar shadows were in their place, the same as on every night, and if it was easy to understand what the women were doing there, and what they were waiting for, it was much more difficult to work out what reasons some men could have for hanging about, doing nothing, in the darkness and cold. They were not all looking for temporary company. Nor had they all got appointments. Among them were men of all races and all ages, who emerged in the evenings, like rats from a hole, to make bold on the fringe of their territories.

The neon sign of the Grelot shed a violet light on a strip of pavement, and from the taxi Maigret could hear muffled music, or rather rhythmic sounds accompanied by a low stamping noise. A short distance away two policemen in uniform were on duty under a lamp post, and at the door, apparently taking the air, was a midget who shot inside as soon as Maigret stepped out of his cab.

In such places it is always like that. The inspector had not yet made his entrance when two men rushed out, and, jostling past him, made off for the darker depths of the district. At the bar, others turned away their heads as he passed, in the hope of not being recognized, and as soon as his back was turned, slipped out also.

Short and thickset, the proprietor came forward.

'If it is Pierrot you are looking for, Inspector . . .'

He was talking loudly on purpose, emphasizing the word inspector, in order to warn everyone in the room. Here too the lighting was violet, and it was hard to make out the customers seated at the tables and in the boxes, for only the dance-floor was illuminated; the faces were lit only by the reflection of the spotlights, which gave them a ghostly appearance.

The band went on playing, the couples dancing, but talk had stopped and all eyes were turned upon the bulky outlines of Maigret who was looking round for a table.

'You would like a seat?'

'Yes.'

'This way, Inspector.'

In saying this, the proprietor had the air of a huckster putting across his patter in front of the painted canvas of his booth at a fair.

'What will you have? It's my round.'

Maigret had expected all this, as he came in. He was used to it.

'A *marc*.'

'An old *marc* for Inspector Maigret!'

On their hanging platform, the four members of the band were dressed in black trousers and dark red silk shirts with long flowing sleeves. They had managed to replace Pierrot, for someone was playing the saxophone, doubling with the accordion.

'Do you want to talk to me?'

Maigret shook his head and pointed to the platform.

'The band?'

'The one who knows Pierrot best.'

'In that case, it's Louis, the accordionist. He's the conductor. In a quarter of an hour's time there's an interval, so he could join you shortly. I suppose you're not in a hurry?'

Five or six persons, including one of the dancers, found it necessary to seek some fresh air. Calmly looking about him, Maigret paid no attention to them, and gradually people began to resume their conversations.

He recognized a number of girls, but they had not come here to pick up customers. They came to dance, mostly with their steadies, and they were wholly rapt up in the dancing, which was for them like a holy rite. Some of them had their eyes closed, as if in ecstasy, others were dancing cheek to cheek with their partners, but with their bodies hardly touching.

There were typists and shop-girls, as well, who had come simply to listen to the band and to dance, and no sightseers were to be seen, nor, as in most night-clubs, couples on the spree, slumming amid the mob.

In the whole of Paris there were not more than two or three dance-halls like this, generally frequented only by regulars, and where much more lemonade was drunk than alcohol.

The four members of the band, up above, looked down upon Maigret with inscrutable expressions; it was impossible to guess their thoughts. The accordionist was a handsome dark young fellow of about thirty who looked like a film star, and who had grown Spanish-style side-whiskers.

A man with a large bag attached to his apron was collecting bills.

Couples waited on the floor. There was one more dance, this time a tango, for which the spotlights changed from violet to red, fading out the girls' make-up and dimming the musicians' shirts; eventually the band put down their instruments and the proprietor, from below, said a few words to the accordionist named Louis.

The latter glanced once more at Maigret's table and decided to come down the ladder.

'You may sit down,' said the inspector.

'We start again in ten minutes.'

'That will be long enough. What will you have?'

'Nothing.'

Silence ensued. From the other tables people were watching them. The bar was crowded, for the most part with men. In some boxes only the girls remained, re-touching their make-up.

Louis spoke first.

'You're barking up the wrong tree,' he observed with bitterness.

'About Pierrot?'

'Pierrot didn't kill Lulu. But it's always the same old thing.'

'Why did he disappear?'

'He's no more a fool than the next man. He knows that he's bound to catch it. How would you like to be arrested?'

'He's a friend of yours?'

'A friend of mine, yes. Probably I know him better than anyone.'

'Perhaps you know where he is?'

'If I knew, I wouldn't say.'

'Do you know?'

'No. I haven't had news of him since we shut down last night. You've seen the papers?'

Louis's voice shook with repressed anger.

'People imagine that because a chap plays in a band he must be a hoodlum. Perhaps you think that, too?'

'No.'

'You see that big fair fellow who plays the drums? Believe it or not, he's taken his *bachot* and even been to the university. His parents are well-off. He's here because he likes it, and next week he's getting married to a girl who's studying medicine. I'm married, too, in case you're interested; I have two children, my wife is expecting a third, and we live in a four-room flat in the Boulevard Voltaire.'

Maigret knew it was true. Louis was forgetting that the inspector knew his kind of people almost as well as he did.

'Why didn't Pierrot get married?' he asked in lowered tones.

'That's another story.'

'Lulu didn't want to?'

'I didn't say so.'

'Some years ago Pierrot was arrested for being a pimp.'

'I know.'

'Well?'

'I tell you again, that's another story.'

'What story?'

'You wouldn't understand. In the first place, he comes from a public orphanage. Does that mean anything to you?'

'Certainly.'

'When he was sixteen, they slung him out on the streets, and he did the best he could. In his place I might have done worse things. As for me, I had my parents, like most people, and I still have.'

He was proud of being a man like any other, but at the same time he felt the need to defend those on the other side of the fence, and Maigret could not help smiling in sympathy.

'What are you smiling at?'

'Because I know all that.'

'If you knew Pierrot, you wouldn't be setting all your cops on his heels.'

'How do you know that the police are after him?'

'The papers don't invent from nothing what they print. And you can feel the backwash in the district. When you see certain faces, you know what that means.'

Louis did not like the police. He did not conceal it.

'There was a time when Pierrot acted the tough,' he went on.

'But he wasn't one?'

'Would you believe me, if I swore he is shy and romantic? Yes, it's a fact.'

'He was in love with Lulu?'

'Yes.'

'He knew her when she was on the streets?'

'Yes.'

'And he let her stay on the streets.'

'What else could he have done? I told you that you wouldn't understand!'

'Then he allowed her to take a steady lover and be kept by him?'

'That's different.'

'Why?'

'Do you need telling how little he had to offer her? Do you imagine he could make a living for her on what he earns here?'

'You keep your family, don't you?'

'Wrong again! My wife is a seamstress; she works ten hours a day and looks after the children, too. What you don't understand is that if you're born in the district and have never known any other . . .'

He broke off.

'Only four minutes left.'

The other members of the band watched them closely from up above, their faces expressionless.

'What I do know is that he didn't kill her. And if he didn't take her away from the claws of her doctor . . .'

'So you know who Lulu's steady lover was?'

'So what?'

'Was it Pierrot who told you?'

'Everybody knows it started in the hospital. Now I'm going to tell you what Pierrot's view was. She had the chance to escape once and for all, to have an easy life and be sure of tomorrow. That's why he said nothing.'

'And Lulu?'

'She must have had her reasons.'

'What reasons?'

'That's no business of mine.'

'What sort of a girl was she?'

Louis looked at the women around them with an expression that suggested that she was no different from the rest.

'She had had a hard life,' he remarked as if that explained everything. 'She wasn't happy down there.'

By 'down there' he evidently meant the far-off Etoile district, which seen from here seemed another world.

'Now and again she came dancing here.'

'Did she look sad?'

Louis shrugged his shoulders. Could the word have any meaning in the La Chapelle district? Were there any really happy girls around them? Even the shop-girls, as they danced, wore a melancholy air and requested plaintive tunes.

'We have a minute left. After that, if you still need me, you will have to wait half an hour.'

'Did Pierrot say anything to you when he came back from the Avenue Carnot last night?'

'He apologized, and spoke of important news, without saying what it was.'

'Was he gloomy?'

'He's always gloomy.'

'Did you know that Lulu was pregnant?'

Louis looked at him hard, at first unbelieving, then astonished, and finally solemn.

'You're sure of that?'

'The medical examiner who performed the autopsy could not have made a mistake.'

'How many months?'

'Six weeks.'

This sank in, perhaps because he had children, and his wife was expecting another. He beckoned to the waiter who stood near them trying to overhear what they were saying.

'Fetch me a drink, Ernest. Anything will do.'

He had forgotten that the minute was up. From the bar the proprietor was observing them.

'I hadn't expected that.'

'Nor had I,' Maigret admitted.

'I suppose the Professor is too old?'

'Men have had children at the age of eighty.'

84

'If what you say is true, that's another reason why he couldn't have killed her.'

'Listen to me, Louis.'

The latter looked at him with some suspicion still, but he was no longer aggressive.

'It may happen that you will get word of Pierrot. In one way or another. I am not asking you to "finger" him. Only to tell him that I should like to talk to him, wherever he wants and whenever he wants. You understand?'

'And you'll let him go?'

'I am not saying I'm going to call off the inquiries. All I promise is that he'll leave me freely.'

'What do you want to ask him?'

'I don't know yet.'

'You still think he killed Lulu?'

'I have no opinion.'

'I don't think he will send word to me.'

'But if he does. . . .'

'I'll pass on your message. Now, if you'll excuse me. . . .'

Draining his glass at one gulp, he climbed up to the platform and buckled the accordion straps round his waist and shoulders. The men in the band asked no questions. He bent over them but it was only to give them the title of the next number. From the bar the men were looking over the girls who were sitting out, and making up their minds which to pick as partners.

'Waiter!'

'There's nothing to pay. It's on the house.'

It was no use arguing. He rose and made for the door.

'Have you found out anything new?'

There was a touch of irony in the proprietor's voice.

'Thank you for the *marc*.'

It was useless to look for a taxi in the neighbourhood, and Maigret reached the Boulevard de la Chapelle, brushing aside the girls who did not recognize him and were trying to pick him up. Three hundred yards away shone the lights of the Barbès crossroads. A fog like the morning's began to fall over the city, and car lights were encircled with a halo.

The Rue Riquet was a few steps farther. He was not long turning into it, where he found Inspector Lober, a man of nearly his own age but who had never been promoted, leaning against a wall smoking a cigarette.

'Anything fresh?'

'Plenty of couples go in and come out, but I haven't seen him.'

Maigret wanted to send Lober home to bed. He also could have telephoned Janvier and told him to go home. And called off the watch in the stations, for he was convinced that Pierrot would not try to leave Paris. But he was compelled to follow routine. He had no right to run any risks.

'You aren't cold?'

Lober already smelt of rum. So long as the *bistrot* on the corner stayed open, he wouldn't do badly. That, indeed, was the reason why all his life he would remain a plain detective.

'Good night, old man. If anything happens, telephone me at home.'

It was eleven o'clock. The crowds were beginning to pour out of the cinemas. Couples on the pavement were walking arm in arm, some women clasping their companion's waist; in corners and doorways some pairs stood clinging together, others were running to catch their bus.

Behind the lighted Boulevards, each side street had its own mystery and its shadows; each one, too, had somewhere or other the yellowing signs of a hotel or two.

It was for the lights that he was making, and at the Barbès crossing he entered a brilliantly illuminated bar where some fifty people were crowded round a huge copper counter.

Though he had meant to order a rum, he said automatically, because of what he had drunk at the Grelot:

'A *marc*.'

Lulu had hung about here, as other girls hung about now, on the look-out for a man's glance.

He walked to the telephone booth, slipped a counter into the instrument and dialled the number of the Quai des Orfèvres. He did not know who was on duty, but recognized the voice of one Lucien, a new man, who had taken his training very seriously and was already preparing for his examinations in order to qualify for promotion.

'Maigret here. Anything new?'

'No, sir. Only that two Arabs have just had a

fight with knives in the Rue de la Goutte d'Or. One of them died the minute he was placed on a stretcher. The other, who was wounded, managed to get away.'

It was no more than three hundred yards from where he stood. It had happened hardly twenty minutes ago, probably while he was walking along the Boulevard de la Chapelle. He had known nothing about it, had heard nothing. The murderer might have passed him by. Before the night ended, other dramas would be played out in the district, one or two of which would come to the notice of the police, but others for long afterwards would remain undetected.

Pierrot, too, was holed up somewhere between Barbès and La Villette.

Did he know that Lulu was pregnant? Was it to tell him about it that she had called the Grelot to ask him out to see her?

Dr. Paul had said six weeks. That meant that for some days past she must have had her suspicions.

Had she disclosed them to Etienne Gouin?

It was possible, but not probable. She was more the kind of girl who would consult a local doctor or a midwife.

Maigret could only go by guess-work. Back at the flat she must have waited a while before making up her mind. According to Madame Gouin, the Professor had looked in on Lulu after dinner but had stayed only a few minutes.

Going back to the bar, Maigret ordered another drink. He had no desire to leave just yet.

This seemed to him the best spot in which to think about Lulu and Pierrot.

'She didn't talk to Gouin,' he murmured.

Pierre Eyraud was the one she would have confided in, which explained his hurried visit.

In that case, would he have killed her?

First, one had to be sure that she knew about her condition. Had she been living in a different district, he would have been positive that she had seen a local doctor. At the Etoile, where she remained a stranger, it was less likely.

Next morning he would have to circulate a notice to all the doctors and midwives in Paris. This seemed most important. Since Dr. Paul's telephone call, he was convinced that Lulu's pregnancy was the key to the affair.

Would Gouin be peacefully asleep? Or was he taking advantage of an evening off to work on some article of surgery?

It was too late to go and see the charwoman, Madame Brault, who lived not far away in the neighbourhood of the Place Clichy. Why had she not mentioned the Professor? Spending as she did every morning in the flat, was it credible that she should be unaware of the identity of Lulu's lover?

They exchanged gossip. In the whole house Madame Brault was the only person who could have understood the secrets of a Louise Filon.

The concierge, to begin with, had kept silent because she owed a debt of gratitude to the Professor and because she must be more or less consciously in love with him.

In fact, it might be said that all the women were striving to protect him, and not the least interesting feature of the case was the power exercised over them by this man of sixty-two.

He made no attempt to charm them. He merely made use of them, almost absent-mindedly, for the sake of physical release, and not one of them bore him a grudge for his cynicism.

Maigret would have to interview the woman assistant, Lucile Decaux. And also, perhaps, Madame Gouin's sister, who was the only one the Professor had apparently failed to captivate.

'How much?'

He took the first taxi.

'Boulevard Richard Lenoir.'

'I know, Monsieur Maigret.'

That reminded him to inquire for the taxi in which Gouin had driven home last evening from the hospital.

He felt sluggish, heavy with the *marc* he had drunk, and he half-closed his eyes as the lights flashed by on both sides of the cab.

He kept coming back to Lulu, and in the darkness of the taxi he pulled his wallet out of his pocket in order to look at her photographs. Her mother had not smiled, either, when she went to have her picture taken.

5

NEXT morning he had an unpleasant aftertaste of *marc* in his mouth. When, in conference at about nine-fifteen, he was told he was wanted on the telephone, he was under the impression that his breath still smelt of stale alcohol and he tried not to talk too closely to his colleagues.

As on every morning, the departmental heads were present, in the office of the P.J.'s Director, whose windows looked out on the Seine; all of them were clutching pretty bulky files. It was a grey day, the river was a dirty colour, and people were walking fast, as on the day before, especially when crossing the windswept Pont Saint-Michel, where men lifted their arms to hold on to their hats, and women reached down to hold in their skirts.

'You can take the call in here.'

'I am afraid it will be a long one, sir. I had better go back to my office.'

Though the others had probably not drunk *marc* the night before, they looked no better than he did, and everyone seemed to be in a bad temper. It must have been the effect of the light.

'Is that you, Chief?' Janvier asked in a voice in which Maigret detected a note of excitement.

'What's happened?'

'He's just come by. Shall I give it you in detail?'

Probably Janvier, too, who had slept on the sofa in Lulu's flat, was looking tired and ill.

'Go on.'

'Here it is. It was a few minutes ago, ten at the most. I was in the kitchen, drinking some coffee I'd made. I had my coat and tie off. I ought to say that it was very late last night before I managed to go to sleep.'

'Did you have a quiet night?'

'I didn't hear anything. It was just that I couldn't sleep.'

'Proceed.'

'You will see, it's quite simple. So simple that I can't quite get over it. I heard a slight noise, a key turning in the lock. I stood still, in a position from which I could observe the sitting-room. Someone entered the vestibule, crossed it and opened the inner door. It was the Professor, who is taller and thinner than I had expected. He was wearing a long dark overcoat, a woollen scarf round his neck, hat on head, and gloves in hand.'

'What did he do?'

'Exactly. That's what I was coming to. He did

nothing. He walked forward a few paces, slowly, like a man entering his home. I wondered for a moment what he was gazing at so intently, and I realized it was at my shoes which I had left on the carpet. Turning his head, he saw me and frowned. Just slightly. He wasn't startled. He didn't seem to be either embarrassed or alarmed.

'He looked at me like someone whose thoughts are elsewhere and who needs a moment to return to reality. Eventually, without raising his voice, he asked:

' "You're from the police?"

'I was so surprised by his appearance, and by the way in which he was taking things, that all I could do was nod.

'For a whole minute both of us were silent, and by the way in which he looked at my stockinged feet I got the impression that he was annoyed by my casualness. But that is only an impression. He may not have noticed my feet.

'I finally said:

' "What were you going to do, Professor?"

' "So you know who I am?"

'That man makes you feel as if you don't exist, and even when he fixes his eyes on you that you have no more importance for him than the pattern on the wallpaper.

' "I was going to do nothing in particular," he muttered. "Just have a look around."

'And he did look around, observing the sofa where the pillow and quilt were lying which I had used, and sniffing the smell of coffee.

'In an impersonal voice, he went on:

' "I am surprised that your chief has not had the curiosity to interview me. You may tell him, young man, that I am at his service. I am now going to Cochin where I shall remain until eleven o'clock. Before returning for lunch I shall visit the Saint-Joseph clinic, and this afternoon I have an important operation at the American Hospital at Neuilly."

'He took one more look around, turned and went out, shutting both doors behind him.

'I opened the window to watch him leave. A taxi was parked outside the house, and on the pavement a young woman with a black brief-case under her arm was waiting for him. She opened the cab-door and got in after him.

'I suppose that when she calls for him in the morning, she telephones from the lodge to say that she is down below.

'That's all, Chief.'

'Thank you very much.'

'Do you think he is well off?'

'He is reported to make a lot of money. He operates free on poor patients, but when he asks a fee it is a stiff one. Why do you ask?'

'Because last night, when I couldn't sleep, I made an inventory of the young woman's effects. It was not what I expected to find. There are indeed two fur coats, but second-rate and one of them sheep-skin. Not a single item, from lingerie to shoes, came from a first-class shop. They aren't, of course, the kind of clothes she used to wear in the Barbès district, but no more are they the clothes you expect to find in the home of a woman kept by a wealthy man. I didn't find a cheque book, nor any document indicating that she had a bank account. Yet, there are only a few thousand-franc notes in her handbag and two more in the drawer of the bedside table.'

'I think you can come back. Have you a key?'

'I saw one in her handbag.'

'Close the door. Fix a thread, or something, across it so that we shall know if it has been opened. Has the charwoman turned up?'

The night before he had not told her whether or not she should come in to clean the flat. No one had considered that she had not been paid her wages.

It was not worth going back to the Director's room, where the conference was over. Lober, in the Rue Riquet, would be tired and perished with cold; probably, since the *bistrots* had opened, he would have warmed himself with a few rums.

Maigret called the Goutte d'Or station.

'Is Janin there? Not in yet? Maigret here. Would you send someone to the Rue Riquet where they will find one of my men, Lober. Tell him that unless there's been a new development he is to telephone his report and get some sleep.'

He did his best to recall the various things that on his way back from Barbès last night he had decided to do this morning. He telephoned Lucas.

'How are things?'

'All right, Chief. At one time last night two patrolling police on bikes in the XXth *arrondisse-*

ment thought they had laid hands on Pierrot. They took the man to the station. He wasn't Pierrot, but a young man much like him, and who, as it happens, is also a musician, in a brasserie in the Place Blanche.'

'I should like you to telephone Béziers. Try to find out whether a certain Ernest Filon, who was in the town hospital some years ago, is still living in the district.'

'Very good.'

'I also want to have the taxi-drivers questioned who generally park in the evenings around Cochin. One of them, the day before yesterday, must have driven the Professor home.'

'Anything else?'

'That's all for now.'

All this was part of the routine. On his desk a large pile of papers was awaiting his signature, besides the reports of the medical examiner and of Gastine-Renette which he ought to pass on to the coroner's court.

He broke off work to ask for the number of his friend Pardon, who was a doctor, and whom he saw pretty regularly once a month.

'Busy?'

'Four or five patients in the waiting-room. Fewer than usual at this time of year.'

'Do you know Professor Gouin?'

'He has operated on several patients of mine, and I have been present at the operations.'

'What is your view of him?'

'He is one of the greatest of doctors, not only that we now have, but that we have ever had.

Unlike many surgeons, he is not merely a hand, but a brain; and we owe him a number of discoveries that are very important, and always will be.'

'But as a man?'

'What do you want to know, exactly?'

'Your opinion.'

'It is hard to say. He is pretty stand-offish, especially with small local doctors such as myself. It seems he keeps his distance with the others too.'

'He's not liked?'

'People are rather afraid of him. He has a certain way of replying to the questions that people are bold enough to put to him. Apparently he's tougher still with some of his patients. There's a story of an extremely rich old lady who begged him to operate on her, offering him a small fortune to do so. Do you know what he answered?

' "The operation would give you an extra fortnight, perhaps a month. The time that I spent on it might save the whole life of another patient."

'Then again, the staff at Cochin worship him.'

'Especially the women?'

'You've heard about that? Apparently in that direction he's almost a case. Sometimes immediately after an operation, he . . . You follow?'

'Yes. Is that all?'

'He's none the less a great and fine man.'

'Thanks, old chap.'

Without quite knowing why, he wanted to have a chat with Désirée Brault. He could have summoned her to him or had her fetched. That is the way in which most of the departmental heads did their work, some of them never leaving the office throughout the day.

He looked in on Lucas, who was busy telephoning.

'I am going out for an hour or two.'

He took one of the official cars and had himself driven to the Rue Nollet, behind the Place Clichy, where Lulu's charwoman lived. It was a dilapidated block, that had not seen a coat of paint in twenty years, and the families packed into it brimmed over on to the landings and on to the staircase, where the children were playing.

Madame Brault lived on the fourth floor, on the courtyard side. There was no lift, the stairs were steep, and Maigret had to stop several times on his way up, sniffing more or less unpleasant odours.

'What is it?' a voice shouted when he knocked. 'Come in. I can't get to the door.'

She was in the kitchen, in her underclothes, with bare feet, washing laundry in a galvanized iron basin. The sight of the inspector did not seem to surprise her. She offered no greeting and waited for him to speak.

'I just looked in as I was passing by.'

'I bet you did!'

Because of the washing, steam covered the windows, through which nothing outside was visible. Sounds of snoring could be heard from the next room, where Maigret caught a glimpse of the foot of a bed; Madame Brault shut the door.

'My husband's asleep,' she said.

'Drunk?'

'Same as ever.'

'Why didn't you tell me yesterday who was Lulu's steady lover?'

'Because you didn't ask me. I remember very well, you asked me if I'd ever seen a man in her flat.'

'And you've never seen him?'

'No.'

'But you knew that it was the Professor?'

By her expression, it was plain that she knew a great deal more than that. Only she was determined to say nothing, unless obliged and coerced. Not because, on her part, she had anything to hide. Nor even, probably, in order to shield someone else. It was simply a matter of principle with her not to help the police; and this was, on the whole, natural enough, considering that they had harried her all her life. She just did not like policemen. They were her natural enemies.

'Did your employer ever discuss him?'

'That happened.'

'What did she tell you about him?'

'She told me so many things!'

'Did she want to leave him?'

'I don't know whether she wanted to leave him, but she was not happy in that house.'

Without being invited, he had sat down in a chair with a straw bottom that creaked.

'What prevented her leaving?'

'I never asked her.'

'Was she in love with Pierrot?'

'It certainly looked like it.'

'Did she get much money from Gouin?'

'He gave her some whenever she asked.'

'Did she ask him often?'

'Whenever there was none in the house. Sometimes when I was about to go shopping I'd find only a few small notes in her bag and in the drawer. I'd tell her about it and she would reply:

' "I'll ask for some." '

'Did she give any to Pierrot?'

'That's no business of mine. If she had been cleverer . . .'

She fell silent.

'What would she have done?'

'First she should never have moved into that house, where she lived like a prisoner.'

'He didn't let her go out?'

'For the most part, it was she who didn't dare go out, in case the gentleman should take it into his head to bid her a good morning as he passed by. She wasn't her own mistress, but a sort of servant, with the difference that she was not expected to work but to go to bed. If she had kept up a flat somewhere else, and if he had been the one who had to go out of his way . . . But what's the use of all this? What exactly do you want from me?'

'A piece of information.'

'Today you want information, and you take your hat off. Tomorrow if I had the bad luck to stop beside a show case, you'd run me into gaol. What information?'

She was hanging the washing up to dry on a cord across the kitchen.

'Did you know that Lulu was pregnant?'

She turned round quickly.

'Who told you that?'

'The autopsy.'

'So she hadn't made a mistake.'

'When did she tell you?'

'About three days before she was shot.'

'She wasn't sure?'

'No. She hadn't yet gone to a doctor. She was afraid of going.'

'Why?'

'For fear, I suppose, of being disappointed.'

'She wanted a child?'

'I think she was glad to be pregnant. But it was still too early to celebrate. I told her that doctors today have a dodge by which they can tell for certain even at two or three weeks.'

'Did she go to consult one?'

'She asked me if I knew one and I gave her the address of someone I know, near here, in the Rue des Dames.'

'Do you know if she saw him?'

'If she did, she didn't tell me.'

'Did Pierrot know?'

'Don't you know anything about women? Have you ever met a woman who told a man about things like that before she was sure?'

'You think she didn't speak to the Professor, either?'

'Use your own gumption.'

'What would have happened, do you think, if she hadn't been murdered?'

'I don't read tea leaves.'

'Would she have kept the child?'

'Of course.'

'Would she have stayed with the Professor?'

'Unless she had gone off with Pierrot.'

'Who did she think was the father?'

Once again she looked at him as if he couldn't tell chalk from cheese.

'You don't imagine it was the old man?'

'It could be.'

'You read about that sort of thing in the papers. But as women are not kept locked up in a stable like cows, and led to the bull once a year, it's hard to swear to whatever it might be.'

Her husband in the next room shifted in bed and groaned. She opened the door.

'In a minute, Jules. I've got someone here. I'll bring your coffee in a minute.'

Turning to Maigret, she added:

'Any more questions?'

'Not exactly. Do you hate Professor Gouin?'

'I've never seen him, I said.'

'But, all the same, you do hate him?'

'I hate all people like that.'

'Supposing that when you arrived that morning you had found in Lulu's hand or on the carpet, within her reach, a revolver. Wouldn't you have been tempted to get rid of it, in order to remove the possibility of suicide and put the Professor under suspicion?'

'You make me tired. Do you think I'm fool enough not to know that when the police have a choice between a big shot and a poor bastard of a musician like Pierrot, it's the poor bastard they'll go for?'

She poured some coffee into a bowl, added sugar, and shouted to her husband:

'Coming.'

Maigret did not persist. Only in the doorway did he turn round to ask the name and address of the doctor in the Rue des Dames.

He was a certain Duclos. He had not been long settled in the practice, and had probably just completed his studies, for his consulting-room was nearly bare, with merely the indispensable instruments bought second-hand. When Maigret told him who he was, the doctor at once showed his awareness.

'I suspected somebody would come one day or another.'

'She gave you her name?'

'Yes. I filled in a form for her.'

'How long had she known she was pregnant?'

The doctor looked more like a student, and to give himself importance he consulted his almost empty filing cabinet.

'She came on Saturday, recommended by a woman I looked after.'

'Madame Brault, I know.'

'She told me that she thought she was pregnant and wanted to be sure.'

'One moment. Did she seem worried?'

'I can assure you that she wasn't. When a girl

of her sort puts that question to me, I always expect her to ask me if I'll do what's necessary to induce an abortion. That happens twenty times a week. I don't know whether it is the same in other districts. In short, I examined her. I asked for the usual sample of urine. She wanted to know what happened next, and I told her about the rabbit test.'

'What was her reaction?'

'She was anxious to know whether we had to kill the rabbit. I told her to come back on Monday afternoon.'

'And she came?'

'At half past five. I informed her that she was well and truly pregnant, and she thanked me.'

'She didn't say anything else?'

'She was insistent, and I assured her it was an absolute certainty.'

'Did she seem happy about it?'

'I'd swear she was.'

On Monday, therefore, about six o'clock, Lulu had left the Rue des Dames and returned to the Avenue Carnot. Towards eight, after dinner, the Professor, according to Madame Gouin, had spent a few minutes in the third-floor flat, and then proceeded to the hospital.

Until around ten, Louise Filon had been at home alone. She had eaten tinned lobster and drunk a little wine. Then, apparently, she went to bed, which had been found unmade—not in disorder, as if she had been sleeping with a man, but simply unmade.

During that period Pierrot was already at the Grelot and she could have telephoned him immediately. Instead, she had not called until about nine-fifteen.

Was it to tell him her news that she had fetched him out to the Etoile during his working hours? If so, why had she delayed so long?

Had Pierrot jumped into a taxi? According to the concierge he had stayed about twenty minutes in the flat.

Gouin, according to the concierge and also according to his wife, had returned from the hospital a little after eleven and had not visited his mistress.

Next morning, at eight, Madame Brault, starting her job, had found Louise dead on the sitting-room sofa, and she maintained that there was no weapon near the body.

Doctor Paul, always cautious in his conclusions, placed the time of death between nine and eleven. Because of the telephone call to the Grelot, nine-thirty could be substituted for nine.

As for the finger-prints taken in the flat, they belonged to four people only: Lulu herself, the charwoman, the Professor and Pierre Eyraud. Moers had sent someone to Cochin to photograph Gouin's prints on a hospital form he had just signed. The other three sets had caused no trouble, for they were all on record in the P.J.

Lulu had evidently not been expecting an attack, since someone had been able to shoot her point-blank.

The flat had not been ransacked, which meant that the murderer had not killed for money, nor to lay his hands on papers of any sort.

'Thank you, Doctor. I suppose that after her appointment no one called to question you about her? Nobody telephoned to discuss her affairs with you?'

'No. When I saw in the paper that she'd been murdered, I expected a visit from the police, given that her charwoman had sent her to me and that she must be in the know. To tell you the truth, if you hadn't come this morning, I was intending to put through a call to you this afternoon.'

A few minutes later, from a *bistrot* in the Rue des Dames, Maigret was telephoning Madame Gouin. She recognized his voice and did not sound surprised.

'Yes, Inspector.'

'You told me yesterday that your sister works in a library. May I ask which one?'

'The municipal library in the Place Saint-Sulpice.'

'Thank you.'

'Have you found out anything?'

'Only that Louise Filon was pregnant.'

'Oh!'

He was sorry he had said this over the wire, for he could not judge her reaction.

'Does that surprise you?'

'Well . . . yes . . . . It's probably silly, but one never expects that to happen to certain kinds of women. One forgets that they are built the same as others.'

'Do you know if your husband was aware of it?'

'He would have spoken to me.'

'Has he ever had a child?'

'Never.'

'He didn't want one?'

'I don't think he cares one way or the other. The fact is that we haven't had one. Very likely because of me.'

The little black car drove him to the Place Saint-Sulpice, which for some reason was the Paris square he disliked most. There he always felt as if he were in some place in the provinces. To his eyes, even the shops appeared different from elsewhere, and the passers-by seemed more sluggish and depressed.

The library was gloomier still, badly lit, and quiet as an empty church; at that time of day only three or four people, regulars probably, were consulting the dusty volumes.

Antoinette Ollivier, Madame Gouin's sister, watched him approach; she looked more than her fifty years, and she had the rather disdainful assurance of women who think they have penetrated all the great truths of life.

'I am Inspector Maigret of the *Police Judiciaire*.'

'I recognized you from your pictures.'

As in a church, she was speaking in low tones. But it reminded him more of school than of a church, when she made him sit down in front of a table covered in green baize which served as her desk. She was fleshier than her sister Germaine, but it was a scarcely living flesh, and her complexion was of a neutral tint such as nuns sometimes have.

'I suppose you are here to put some questions to me?'

'Quite right. Your sister informed me that you paid her a visit yesterday evening.'

'So I did. I arrived about half past eight, and left at half past eleven, as soon as the individual you know had come in.'

For her, it must have represented the height of contempt to avoid mentioning even the name of her brother-in-law, and she seemed very pleased by the word 'individual', in which she carefully drew out all the syllables.

'Do you often happen to spend an evening with your sister?'

For some reason or another, Maigret suspected that she was on her guard and that she would be even more reticent than the concierge or Madame Brault.

The other two had replied with caution, because they were afraid of incriminating the Professor.

This woman, on the contrary, was probably afraid of exonerating him.

'Not very often,' she said regretfully.

'Does that mean once every six months, once a year, or once every two years?'

'Perhaps once a year.'

'You had made an appointment with her?'

'One doesn't make appointments with one's sister.'

'You went out there without knowing whether she would be at home? Haven't you a telephone in your flat?'

'Yes.'

'Didn't you call your sister?'

'She called me.'

'To ask you to go and see her?'

'Not exactly. She talked about one thing and another.'

'What things?'

'Mostly about the family. She doesn't write often. And I am in touch with our brothers and sisters.'

'She said she would like to see you?'

'More or less. She asked me if I was free.'

'What time was that?'

'About half past six. I had just got home and had started cooking.'

'You weren't surprised?'

'No. I merely made certain that HE was not going to be in. What has HE told you?'

'You are referring to Professor Gouin?'

'Yes.'

'I haven't interviewed him yet.'

'Because you think he is innocent? Because he's a famous surgeon, a member of the Academy of Medicine and because . . .'

Without raising her voice, her tone had become more resonant.

'What happened,' he interrupted, 'when you reached the Avenue Carnot?'

'I went up, kissed my sister and took off my coat and hat.'

'Where were you?'

'In the little room, next to Germaine's bed-room, which she calls her *boudoir*. The big sit-ting-room is gloomy and hardly ever used.'

'What did you do?'

'What sisters of our age usually do when they meet again after an interval of some months. We chatted. I gave her the news about everyone. I talked especially about François, a nephew of ours who was ordained a year ago and is about to go to the north of Canada as a missionary.'

'Did you drink anything?'

The question surprised her, startling her to such a degree that she coloured a little.

'First, we had coffee.'

'And then?'

'I sneezed several times. I told my sister I was afraid I had caught cold coming out of the Metro, where it was stifling hot. It was too hot at my sister's, also.'

'Were the servants in the flat?'

'They both went to bed about nine, after say-ing good night. My sister has had the same cook for eleven years. The maids come and go more frequently, for obvious reasons.'

He did not ask her for the reasons, he un-derstood.

'So, you sneezed. . . .'

'Germaine suggested a hot toddy, and went to the kitchen to make it.'

'What did you do while she was out of the room?'

'I read a magazine article about our own village.'

'Was your sister long away?'

'As long as it takes to boil a couple of glasses of water.'

'On previous occasions, did you wait for your brother-in-law to come back before you left?'

'I always tried to avoid meeting him.'

'Were you surprised when you saw him come in?'

'My sister had assured me he would not be back before midnight.'

'How did he look?'

'As he always does, like a man who thinks himself above the ordinary laws of decency and morality.'

'You noticed nothing special about him?'

'I didn't take the trouble to observe him. I put on my hat and coat and went off, banging the door.'

'In the course of the evening, you didn't hear a noise that might have been a shot?'

'No. Until eleven o'clock or so someone in the house on the floor above was playing the piano. I recognized it as Chopin.'

'Did you know that your brother-in-law's mistress was pregnant?'

'It doesn't surprise me.'

'Did your sister mention it?'

'She didn't speak to me about that girl.'

'Did she never discuss her?'

'No.'

'However, you know all about her?'

She blushed.

'She must have referred to her in the beginning, when that individual installed her in the house.'

'Did it weigh on her mind?'

'Everyone has his own ideas. One can't live for years with such a person without something rubbing off.'

'In other words, your sister didn't take her husband to task for this liaison and didn't resent his bringing Louise Filon into the house?'

'What are you driving at?'

He would have had some difficulty in replying to that question. He had a feeling of burrowing forward little by little, without knowing where he would end up, anxious to form a more or less precise conception of the persons connected with Lulu, and of Lulu herself.

They were disturbed by a young man wanting some books, and Antoinette left the inspector for a few minutes. When she returned, she had worked up a fresh store of hatred for her brother-in-law and she gave Maigret no time to open his mouth.

'When are you going to arrest him?'

'You think it was he who killed Louise Filon?'

'Who else could it be?'

'It could be her lover, Pierrot, for instance.'

'What reason would he have?'

'Jealousy, or because she intended to break with him.'

'But do you imagine that the other man wasn't jealous, too? Don't you think that someone of his age would be furious when he saw a girl preferring a younger man to himself? And supposing it was him she'd decided to leave?'

She seemed anxious to hypnotize him, the more surely to plant in his head the idea of the Professor's guilt.

'If you knew him better, you would realize that he is not a man to think twice about eliminating a human being.'

'I thought, on the contrary, that he devoted himself to saving human life.'

'Absolute vanity! To prove to the world that he is the greatest surgeon of the age. The proof is that he only undertakes difficult operations.'

'Perhaps because other doctors can deal with the easy cases.'

'You are defending him, without knowing him.'

'I am trying to understand.'

'It isn't so complicated as all that.'

'You are forgetting that according to the medical examiner, who is seldom wrong, the murder was committed before eleven o'clock. Now, it was after eleven when the concierge saw the Professor come in, and he went up at once to the fourth floor.'

'What is there to prove that he didn't come back for a first time, earlier?'

'I imagine it is simple to check at the hospital on how he spent his time.'

'Have you done so?'

It was Maigret's turn to be on the point of blushing.

'Not yet.'

'Well, you'd better do so! It is probably more worth while than tracking down a young fellow who's done nothing at all.'

'You hate the Professor?'

'Him and all his kind.'

She spoke these words with so much conviction that the three or four readers doing research work simultaneously looked up.

'You have forgotten your hat!'

'I thought I had left it at the entrance.'

With a finger of scorn she pointed to it on the green baize of the table, where the presence of a man's hat probably was for her the height of incongruity.

6

IN a sense, and from the technical point of view, Antoinette had not been far wrong.

When Maigret reached the Cochin hospital in the Faubourg Saint-Jacques, Etienne Gouin had already left with his assistant for the Saint-Joseph Clinic at Passy. As it was after eleven o'clock the inspector was not surprised. It was not to meet the Professor that he had come. Actually, and without quite knowing why, perhaps he did not yet want to confront him?

Gouin's department was on the second floor, and Maigret had to negotiate with the secretariat before he was allowed to go up. He found the long corridor busier than he expected, the nurses working at full pressure. The one he spoke to, as she came out of a ward, looked less anxious than the rest; she was a middle-aged woman with hair already turned white.

'Are you the matron?'

'The day-matron.'

He told who he was and explained that he wanted to put some questions to her.

'What about?'

He was reluctant to admit that it was about the Professor. She had led him to the door of a small office, but did not invite him in.

'Is that the operating theatre at the end of the corridor?'

'One of them, yes.'

'What happens when a surgeon spends part of the night in the hospital?'

'I don't follow. You mean when a surgeon is here to perform an operation?'

'No. Unless I'm mistaken, it sometimes happens that they are here for other reasons; for instance, if they are afraid of complications setting in, or waiting for the results of an operation.'

'Yes, that happens. But what about it?'

'Where do they spend the night?'

'That depends.'

'On what?'

'On how long they are staying. If it is not for long, they use my office or walk about in the corridor. On the other hand, if it is a matter of waiting several hours, in order to be available in case of emergency they go upstairs to the house-doctors' quarters where there are two or three rooms at their disposal.'

'They go up by the stairs?'

'Or they take the lift. The rooms are on the

116

fourth floor. For the most part, they rest until they are called.'

She was obviously wondering what was the point of these questions. The newspapers had not mentioned Gouin's name in connexion with Lulu's death. It was likely that no one here knew about his relations with Pierrot's girl.

'I suppose I couldn't have a talk with someone who was on duty the night before last?'

'After eight o'clock?'

'Yes. I should have said during the night of Monday to Tuesday.'

'The nurses on duty now are in the same position as myself. They belong to the day staff. But possibly one of the house-doctors was on duty. Wait a moment.'

She looked into two or three rooms, and eventually returned with a tall, bony, red-haired young fellow, wearing thick glasses.

'Someone from the police,' she offered before going to sit down in her office, into which she did not invite them.

'Inspector Maigret,' he explained.

'I thought I recognized you. You want some information?'

'Were you here on the night of Monday to Tuesday?'

'A large part of the night. The Professor operated on a child on Monday afternoon. It was a difficult case, and he asked me to keep a close watch on the patient.'

'Didn't he come himself?'

'He spent most of the night in the hospital.'

'Was he on this floor with you?'

'He arrived a little after eight, together with his assistant. We all went in to see the patient, and stayed there, waiting for a development that did not materialize. I suppose you don't want the technical details?'

'I probably shouldn't understand a word of them. You stayed an hour or two with the patient?'

'Less than an hour. Mademoiselle Decaux insisted that the Professor should go and get some rest, for he had operated on an urgent case the night before. Eventually he went to lie down.'

'How was he dressed?'

'He wasn't expecting to operate. Nor did he have to. He was wearing his day-time clothes.'

'Did Mademoiselle Decaux stay with you?'

'Yes. We chatted. A little after eleven the Professor came down. I had been looking in on the patient every fifteen minutes. We went in together once more, and as the crisis seemed to have passed, the Professor decided to go home.'

'With Mademoiselle Decaux?'

'They nearly always come and go together.'

'So that from eight-forty-five until eleven, the Professor was alone on the fourth floor?'

'Alone in a room, at any rate. I can't make out why you are asking these questions.'

'Could he have left without your noticing?'

'By the stairs, yes.'

'Could he have walked past the entrance-desk without attracting attention?'

'It's possible. People don't pay attention to the

comings and goings of the doctors, especially at night.'

'Thank you very much. May I have your name?'

'Mansuy. Raoul Mansuy.'

This was the point on which Madame Gouin's sister had not been so far out. Materially speaking, Etienne Gouin could have left the hospital, been driven to the Avenue Carnot and returned, without anyone having noticed his absence.

'I suppose I may not ask why . . . ?' the housedoctor began just as Maigret was walking away.

The inspector shook his head and went downstairs, crossed the courtyard and found the little black car and P.J. driver waiting by the kerb. When he reached the Quai des Orfèvres, he omitted to cast his usual glance through the windows of the waiting-room. Before entering his office, he walked into the inspectors' room, where Lucas rose to speak to him.

'I have news from Béziers.'

Maigret had almost forgotten Louise Filon's father.

'The man died three years ago of cirrhosis of the liver. Before that he did occasional work in the town slaughterhouses.'

*

No one had so far appeared to claim Louise's estate—if there was one.

*

'A man named Louis has been waiting half an hour to see you.'

'A musician?'

'I think so.'

'Bring him into my office.'

Maigret went in, took off his hat and overcoat, sat down at his desk and picked up one of the pipes stacked beside his blotting-pad. A few moments later, the accordionist was introduced, looking far from easy, and glancing round before he took a seat, as if he expected a trap.

'You may leave us, Lucas.'

And to Louis:

'If it's going to take some time, you had better take off your coat.'

'It's not worth it. He's telephoned.'

'When?'

'This morning, a little after nine.'

He considered the inspector, paused, and asked:

'Does it still hold?'

'What I said yesterday? Certainly. If Pierrot is innocent, he has nothing to fear.'

'He didn't kill her. He would have told me. I passed on your message, explaining that you were prepared to meet him wherever he wanted and that afterwards he would be set at liberty again.'

'Let's make certain we understand one another. I don't want any mistakes. If I think him innocent, he will go entirely free. If I think him guilty, or have any doubts, I promise not to take advantage of our meeting—that is to say, to let him go, but the search for him will be resumed at once.'

'That's more or less what I told him.'

'What did he say?'

'That he's ready to see you. He has nothing to hide.'

'Would he come here?'

'So long as he's not set upon by reporters and photographers. And on condition that he can reach the building without being jumped on by the police.'

Louis was speaking slowly, weighing his words, without taking his eyes off Maigret.

'Can it be arranged quickly?' the inspector asked.

He looked at the time. It was not yet twelve. Between twelve and two o'clock the offices of the Quai des Orfèvres are quiet and almost deserted. It was the time of day that Maigret liked to choose, whenever he could, to conduct a delicate interview.

'He can be here in half an hour.'

'In that case, listen. I suppose he has some money on him. Tell him to take a taxi to the opposite side of the *Dépôt* on the Quai d'Horloge. There are very few people about on the quay. Nobody will pay any attention to him. One of my inspectors will be waiting for him at the gate, and will bring him here through the *Palais de Justice*.'

Louis rose, and looked steadily into Maigret's eyes, conscious of the responsibility he was undertaking in regard to his friend.

'I believe you,' he muttered finally. 'In half an hour, or an hour at the outside.'

When he had left, Maigret telephoned the Brasserie Dauphine to order something to eat.

'Send it up for two. And four half-pints.'

Next he called his wife to warn her that he would not be back for lunch.

Then, in a fit of conscientiousness, he went into the Chief's office, to inform him about the experiment he was about to make.

'You think he's innocent?'

'Until proved otherwise. If he were guilty, there would be no sense in his wanting to see me. Or else, he's devilish tough.'

'The Professor?'

'I don't know. I don't know anything yet.'

'Have you interviewed him?'

'No. Janvier has had a short talk with him.'

The Chief knew it was useless to ask questions. Maigret had the brooding, obstinate look that was well known at the Quai, and at such times he was even less talkative than usual.

'The girl was pregnant,' was all he chose to say, as if this fact particularly bothered him.

Returning to the inspectors' room, he found that Lucas had not yet gone out to lunch.

'I suppose they haven't found the taxi-driver?'

'There's no hope of finding him till this evening. Drivers on nightshift are all in bed now.'

'It wouldn't be a bad idea to look for two taxis.'

'I don't follow.'

'It's conceivable, for instance, that earlier in the evening, a little before ten, the Professor may have been driven to the Avenue Carnot and then returned to hospital.'

'I'll check.'

He was looking round for the detective whom he was to post in front of the *Dépôt* to bring in Pierrot, and he picked young Lapointe.

'Go and station yourself on the pavement opposite the *Dépôt*. At a given moment someone will get out of a taxi. It will be the saxophonist.'

'Is he giving himself up?'

'He's coming to have a talk. Treat him gently. Bring him to me by way of the little courtyard and the corridors of the *Palais*. I have promised that he won't be spotted by the Press.'

Reporters were nearly always prowling about in the corridors, but temporarily it was not hard to dodge them.

When Maigret stepped back into his office, the sandwiches and the beers were waiting for him on a tray. He drank one of the half-pints, but did not eat, whiling away a quarter of an hour on his feet at the window, watching the barges gliding on the grey water.

At last he heard the footsteps of two men, opened the door, and signalled to Lapointe that he could go.

'Come in, Pierrot.'

Pale and with shadows under his eyes, Pierrot was obviously upset. As his friend had done, he began by looking all round like a man who suspects a trap.

'You and I are the only people in the room,' Maigret reassured him. 'You may take off your coat. Give it to me.'

He put it over the back of a chair.

'Have a drink?'

He held out a glass of beer, and took one himself.

'Sit down, I rather thought you would come.'

'Why?'

His voice was hoarse, as of someone who has not slept all night and who has smoked one cigarette after another. Two fingers of his right hand were stained with nicotine. He had not shaved. No doubt, wherever he had gone to earth, he had no opportunity to do so.

'Have you had anything to eat?'

'I am not hungry.'

He looked younger than his years, and he was so nervous that it was exhausting to watch him. Even now that he was sitting down, he still trembled from top to toe.

'You promised . . .' he began.

'I shall keep my word.'

'I've come of my own free will.'

'You were right to do so.'

'I did not kill Lulu.'

Suddenly, when Maigret was least expecting it, he burst into sobs. Very likely it was the first time he had let himself go since he had heard of the death of his girl-friend. He was sobbing like a child, hiding his face with both hands, and the inspector took care not to intervene. In fact, since in the little restaurant on the Boulevard Barbès he had read in the paper that Lulu was dead, he had not had a moment to think about her—only about the threat hanging over his own head.

Within a single moment he had become a hunted man, who at every minute was risking his liberty, if not his life.

Now that he was present in the Quai des Orfèvres, face to face with the police who had been his nightmare, he had abruptly broken down.

'I swear that I didn't kill her. . . .' he repeated.

Maigret believed him. These were not the tones nor the behaviour of a murderer. Louis had been right, the night before, when he had spoken of his friend as a weakling who acted tough.

With his fair hair, blue eyes and almost babyish features, here was no butcher's apprentice; he reminded one rather of an office clerk who could easily be imagined taking a Sunday afternoon stroll in the Champs-Elysées with his wife.

'You really thought it was me?'

'No.'

'Then why did you say so to the papers?'

'I said nothing to the reporters. They write what they like. And in the circumstances . . .'

'I didn't kill her.'

'Take it easy. You may smoke.'

Pierrot's hand was still trembling as he lit his cigarette.

'There is one question I must put to you first of all. When you went to the Avenue Carnot on Monday evening, was Louise still alive?'

Pierrot gaped at him and cried:

'Of course she was!'

It was probably true; otherwise he would not have had to wait for the paper at lunch-time next

125

day to give him a fright and send him into hiding.

'When she telephoned you at the Grelot, did you have any suspicion of what she was going to tell you?'

'I had no idea. She sounded beside herself, and wanted to see me at once.'

'What did you think?'

'That she'd made up her mind.'

'To do what?'

'To ditch it all.'

'Ditch what?'

'The old man.'

'You'd asked her to do so?'

'For two years I'd been begging her to come and live with me.'

With an air of defying the inspector, and the whole world, too, he added:

'I loved her.'

There was no emphasis in his tones. On the contrary, he was clipping his words.

'You're sure you won't have a bite?'

This time Pierrot automatically took a sandwich, and so did Maigret. It was better like this. They both started eating, and the atmosphere relaxed. No noise was to be heard in the offices except for the distant clacking of a typewriter.

'Had it ever happened before that Lulu summoned you to the Avenue Carnot in your working hours?'

'No. Not the Avenue Carnot. Once, when she was still living in the Rue La Fayette and suddenly felt ill. . . . It was only an attack of indi-

126

gestion, but she was frightened. . . . She was always afraid of death. . . .'

Because of that word, and the images it conjured up, his eyes once more filled with tears, and there was a pause before he next took a bite of the sandwich.

'What did she say on Monday evening? One moment. Before you answer, tell me if you have a key to the flat?'

'No.'

'Why not?'

'I don't know. No reason, really. I seldom went to see her there, and when I did she was always at home to let me in.'

'So you rang the bell, and she opened the door.'

'I didn't have to ring. She was looking out for me, and opened the door as soon as I came out of the lift.'

'I thought she had gone to bed.'

'She had done, earlier. She must have telephoned from her bed. But she got up a little before I arrived, and was wearing a dressing-gown.'

'Did she seem in a normal state of mind?'

'No.'

'What was she like?'

'It's hard to say. She looked as if she had been thinking hard and was on the point of making a serious decision. I was frightened when I saw her.'

'What of?'

The musician paused.

'All right,' he muttered eventually, 'I was frightened because of the old man.'

'You mean the Professor when you say that?'

'Yes. I was always afraid he'd decide to get a divorce and marry Lulu.'

'Did the question ever come up?'

'If it did, she didn't mention it to me.'

'Did she want him to marry her?'

'I don't know. I think not.'

'She was in love with you?'

'I think so.'

'You aren't sure?'

'I suppose women are different from men.'

'What do you mean?'

He did not elaborate—possibly because he was incapable of it—and merely shrugged his shoulders.

'She was a poor little thing,' he finally murmured as though to himself.

The food stuck in his throat, but he mechanically kept on eating.

'Where did she sit when you came in?'

'She didn't sit. She was much too excited to sit down. She started pacing up and down and, without looking at me, said:

' "I've some very important news for you."

'Then as if to get it off her chest:

' "I am pregnant." '

'Did she seem glad?'

'Neither glad nor sorry.'

'You thought it was your child?'

He did not venture a reply, but by his attitude it was clear that he thought the answer obvious.

128

'What did you say?'

'Nothing. It made me feel funny. I wanted to take her in my arms.'

'But she didn't let you?'

'No. She went on pacing the room. She was talking to herself, saying more or less:

' "I wonder what I ought to do. This alters everything. It could be very important. If I speak to him about it. . . ." '

'She was alluding to the Professor?'

'Yes. She didn't know whether or not she should tell him the truth. She wasn't sure what his reaction would be.'

And Pierrot, who had finished his sandwich, sighed dejectedly:

'I don't know how to explain it. I remember the smallest details, and yet it's all confused. I hadn't thought it would happen like that.'

'What had you hoped for?'

'That she'd fall into my arms, swearing that at last she'd made up her mind to come to me.'

'But the idea didn't occur to her?'

'Perhaps it did. I'm almost certain it did. She'd always wanted to. In the beginning, when she came out of hospital, she claimed she was obliged to act as she did out of gratitude.'

'She felt she owed a debt to Gouin?'

'He had saved her life. I think he spent more time over her case than over any of his other patients.'

'You believed that?'

'Believed what?'

'In Lulu's sense of gratitude?'

129

'I told her she wasn't compelled to remain his mistress. He had plenty of others.'

'Do you think he was in love with her?'

'He wanted her, for sure. I suppose she'd got under his skin.'

'And you?'

'I loved her.'

'To sum up, why did she ask you round?'

'I wondered, too.'

'It was about half past five at the doctor's in the Rue des Dames that she definitely learnt she was pregnant. Couldn't she have seen you then?'

'Oh yes. She knew where I generally had dinner before turning up at the Grelot.'

'She went home. Later, between seven-thirty and eight the Professor looked in.'

'She spoke to me about that.'

'Did she say whether she'd told him her news?'

'She didn't tell him anything.'

'She had dinner and went to bed. Probably she didn't fall asleep. And around nine she telephoned you.'

'I know. I've been thinking about it all, trying to understand. But so far, I can't make it out. All I know for certain is that I didn't kill her.'

'Tell me frankly, Pierrot: if on Monday evening she had declared that she didn't want to see you any more, would you have killed her?'

The young man looked at him, with the hint of a smile rising to his lips.

'You want me to put the noose round my neck?'

'You don't have to answer.'

'I might perhaps have killed her. But, firstly,

she didn't say that, and secondly I had no revolver.'

'You had one last time you were arrested.'

'That was years ago and the police never gave it me back. I haven't had one since. In any case, I wouldn't have killed her that way.'

'How would you have done it?'

'I don't know. Perhaps I might have struck her without knowing what I was doing, or would I have strangled her?'

He gazed at the parquet floor at his feet and took some time before he added in a more hesitant tone of voice:

'I might have done nothing at all. There are things you think about when you're half asleep, but never carry out.'

'Killing Lulu had occurred to you when you were half asleep?'

'Yes.'

'Because you were jealous of Gouin?'

He shrugged his shoulders again, probably meaning that words were inadequate, and that the truth was much more complicated.

'Before Gouin, you were already Louise Filon's lover, and I think I am right in saying that you did not stop her from walking the streets?'

'That's different.'

Maigret was doing his utmost to come as close to the truth as possible, but he well knew that the absolute truth was beyond reach.

'You've never taken a whack of the Professor's money?'

'Never!' he retorted sharply, with a fierce shake

of the head that suggested he was about to explode with rage.

'Did Louise give you presents?'

'Nothing but trifles, a ring, ties, socks . . .'

'But you accepted them?'

'I didn't want to hurt her feelings.'

'What would you have done if she had left Gouin?'

'We should have lived together.'

'As before?'

'No.'

'Why not?'

'I never liked that sort of life.'

'What would you have lived on?'

'I earn my own living.'

'Not much of a living, so Louis tells me.'

'Not much of one, no. But I didn't expect to stay in Paris.'

'Where were you thinking of going?'

'Anywhere. South America or Canada.'

He was even less mature in mind than Maigret had thought.

'Was Lulu enthusiastic about this idea?'

'Sometimes it appealed to her, and now and again she'd promise that we should set off together in a month or so.'

'I imagine it was in the evening that she talked like that?'

'How do you know?'

'And in the morning she saw things in a different light?'

'She was frightened.'

'What of?'

'Of starving to death.'

In the end, one really came down to it. And an inevitable feeling of resentment was obviously welling up in Pierrot.

'Wouldn't you agree that it was because of this fear of hers that she stayed with the Professor?'

'Possibly.'

'Isn't it true that she'd often gone hungry in the course of her life?'

The young man replied challengingly:

'So have I!'

'But her fear was of starting to starve all over again.'

'What are you trying to prove?'

'Nothing. I am simply trying to understand. One thing is certain: on Monday evening someone shot Lulu at point-blank range. You maintain it was not you, and I believe you.'

'You really do believe me?' Pierrot murmured doubtfully.

'Until I have proof to the contrary.'

'And you'll let me go?'

'As soon as we have finished this interview.'

'You'll call off the search, and tell your men to leave me alone?'

'I shall even allow you to go back to your job at the Grelot.'

'But the papers?'

'I shall issue a communiqué straight away, announcing that you presented yourself to the P.J. of your own free will, and that after the explanations you gave you were set at liberty.'

'That doesn't mean that I'm not still a suspect.'

'I shall add that there is no evidence against you.'

'That's a little better.'

'Did Lulu own a revolver?'

'No.'

'You said just now that she was afraid.'

'Afraid of poverty and life, but not of people. She wouldn't have had any use for a revolver.'

'You stayed a bare quarter of an hour with her on Monday evening?'

'I had to get back to the Grelot. Besides, I did not like being there at a time when the old man might come in at any minute. He has a key.'

'Had that ever occurred?'

'Once.'

'What happened?'

'Nothing. It was in the afternoon when he never usually called at Lulu's. We had made an appointment in town, but something had happened to stop me keeping it. As I was in the neighbourhood, I went up to see her. We were both in the sitting-room, chatting, when we heard the key turn in the lock. He came in. I didn't try to hide. He didn't even look at me. He walked into the middle of the room, with his hat on his head, and stood there without saying a word. It was rather as if I hadn't been a human being.'

'In short you still don't know exactly why Lulu asked you round on Monday night?'

'I suppose she needed to talk to someone.'

'How did your meeting end?'

'She said: "I wanted you to know. I've no idea

what I'm going to do. At any rate, it doesn't show yet. You think about it, too." '

'Had Lulu ever spoken to you of marrying the Professor?'

He looked as if he were racking his memory.

'Once, when we were in a restaurant in the Boulevard Rochechouart and we were talking about a girl we know who had just married. She said: "It all depends on me whether he gets a divorce in order to marry me." '

'Did you believe her?'

'He might have done so. At that age, men are capable of anything.'

Maigret could not repress a smile.

'I am not asking you where you've been hiding since yesterday lunch-time.'

'I wouldn't tell you. Am I free to go?'

'Entirely.'

'If I go out, your men won't arrest me?'

'It might be wise to spend an hour or two in this neighbourhood without making yourself too conspicuous, so that I shall have time to give my orders. There is a Brasserie in the Place Dauphine where you'll be safe.'

'Pass me my coat.'

He seemed much more tired than when he had come in, because he was no longer living on his nerves.

'You would do better still to take a room in the first hotel you come across and go to bed.'

'I shouldn't sleep.'

In the doorway, he turned back.

'What's going to be done?'

Maigret understood.

'If no one comes forward . . .' he began.

'I can claim her?'

'In the absence of family . . .'

'Will you let me know how I ought to go about it?'

He wanted to give Lulu a decent funeral, and no doubt their friends in the dance-hall and in the Barbès district would follow behind the hearse.

Maigret watched his weary figure disappearing down the long corridor, and slowly shut the door; he stood motionless for a while in the middle of his office, and then made for the inspectors' room.

7

I t was about six o'clock when the P.J. car stopped in the Avenue Carnot in front of the block where the Gouins lived, but on the opposite of the road, and headed towards the Ternes district. Night had fallen early, for as on the past three days, the sun had never shone.

The light was on in the concierge's lodge. It was on, too, in the left-hand part of the Gouins' flat on the fourth floor. A few other windows, here and there, were also lit up.

Some of the flats were temporarily unoccupied. The Ottrebons, for instance, who were Belgians and in high finance, were wintering in Egypt. On the second floor, the Comte de Tavera and his family had gone shooting for the season to their château somewhere south of the Loire.

Wedged in the back of the car and hunched

up in his overcoat, with only his pipe protruding through its raised collar, Maigret made no move, and seemed in such an evil temper that after a few moments the driver pulled a newspaper from his pocket, muttering:

'May I?'

It was a wonder how he could read with no more light than the beam of a street-lamp.

All afternoon Maigret had worn the same expression. It was not really bad temper, as his colleagues knew, but the effect was the same, and word had been passed round at the Quai des Orfèvres not to disturb him.

He had hardly left his office, except once or twice to loom up in the inspectors' room where he'd look round heavily, as if he had forgotten what he meant to do.

He had dealt with files that had been pending for weeks with as much zeal as if they had suddenly become extremely urgent. About four-thirty he had called the American Hospital at Neuilly for the first time.

'Is Professor Gouin engaged on an operation?'

'Yes. He won't finish for another hour. Who is wanting him?'

He had hung up, and re-read the report drawn up by Janvier on the tenants in the house and the replies they had made to him. Nobody had heard the shot. On the same floor as Louise, a certain Madame Mattetal occupied the flat on the right; she was a young widow who had spent the evening at the theatre. On the floor below the Crémieux had given a dinner party for ten, which had ended noisily.

Maigret had worked on another case, and made a few unimportant telephone calls.

At half past five, when he had called Neuilly for the second time, he was told that the operation was over and that the Professor was dressing. It was then that he had taken the car.

Not many people were passing along the pavements of the Avenue Carnot, and motors were few. Over the driver's shoulder he could read the newspaper's front-page headline:

'Pierrot-the-Musician Released.'

As he had promised, Maigret had given the news to the reporters. The dashboard clock was dimly luminous, and showed six-twenty. Had there been a *bistrot* nearby he would have got out for a drink and he was sorry he had not stopped on the way.

Not until ten to seven did a taxi stop in front of the block. Etienne Gouin alighted first, and stood still for a moment on the pavement while his assistant followed him out of the cab.

They were near a street-lamp, and his figure was outlined in its light. He must have been half a head taller than Maigret and almost as broad in the shoulders. It was hard to guess his weight, because of his flowing overcoat, which looked too big for him and was cut much longer than was fashionable that year. Obviously he did not bother overmuch about his appearance, and his hat had been put on anyhow.

As he was, he gave the impression of a stout man who had grown thin, and in whose body only the big-boned structure remained.

He waited without showing impatience, gazing absent-mindedly into space, while the young woman drew some money from her bag to pay the driver. Then, as the taxi went off, he stood listening to what she had to say. Probably she reminded him of next day's appointments.

She walked with him as far as the entrance-hall, where she handed him the black leather brief-case she was holding, and watched him enter the lift before she set off towards the Ternes.

'Follow her.'

'Yes, sir.'

The car had only to coast down the slope of the avenue. Lucile Decaux was walking fast, without looking back. She was a small brunette, and so far as could be made out, slightly plump. She turned the corner of the Rue des Acacias, entered a *delicatessen*, then a baker's shop next door, and finally, a hundred yards farther on, a dilapidated-looking block of flats.

Maigret waited ten minutes in his car before he approached the block and addressed the concierge; her lodge was very different from the one in the Avenue Carnot, being cluttered up with a grown-up's bed and a child's cot.

'Mademoiselle Decaux?'

'The fourth floor, on the right. She has just come in.'

There was no lift. On the fourth floor he rang

the doorbell and heard footsteps within. A voice asked from behind the door:

'Who is it?'

'Inspector Maigret.'

'One moment, please.'

The voice betrayed neither surprise nor alarm. Before she let him in, she went into another room, and a few seconds passed before she returned; Maigret saw why when the door was drawn open: she was wearing a dressing-gown and slippers.

'Come in,' she said, eyeing him with interest.

The flat consisted of three rooms and a kitchen; it was extremely clean, and the floor was so highly waxed that it was as easy to slip as on a skating rink. He was shown into a sitting-room which was rather like a studio, with a divan covered in striped material, plenty of books on shelves, a gramophone and shelves loaded with records. Over the fireplace, in which the young woman had just lit a log-fire, was a framed photograph of Etienne Gouin.

'May I take off my coat?'

'Please do. I was just making myself comfortable when you rang the bell.'

She was not pretty. Her features were irregular and her lips too thick, but she seemed to have an attractive figure.

'Am I holding up your dinner?'

'It doesn't matter. Sit down.'

She pointed to an armchair, and herself sat down on the edge of the divan, drawing the skirt of her dressing-gown around her bare legs.

She asked no questions, but studied him as some people study a celebrated person whom they are seeing for the first time in flesh and blood.

'I preferred not to trouble you at the hospital.'

'You would have found it difficult, for I was in the operating theatre.'

'Are you generally present at the Professor's operations?'

'Always.'

'Since when?'

'Ten years ago. Before then I was his pupil.'

'You are a doctor?'

'Yes.'

'May I ask your age?'

'Thirty-six.'

She replied without hesitation, in an almost expressionless voice, but he could sense in it none the less a certain distrust, and perhaps even hostility.

'I have come to clear up a few points of detail. I expect you know that in an investigation such as I am conducting, everything has to be verified.'

She waited for his questions.

'On Monday evening, unless I am mistaken, you went to pick up your chief at the Avenue Carnot, a little before eight?'

'That is true. I kept the taxi waiting and telephoned the Professor from the concierge's lodge to tell him I was waiting.'

'That's your normal procedure?'

'Yes. I only go up to the flat when there is work to do in the office or papers to collect.'

'Where did you stand while the Professor was coming down?'

'In front of the lift-gate.'

'So you know that he stopped on his way down?'

'He stopped a few moments at the third floor. I suppose you know all about it?'

'I do.'

'Why haven't you asked the Professor himself?'

He preferred not to answer.

'Did he behave the same as on any other evening? Was he at all preoccupied?'

'Only over the condition of his patient.'

'Did he say anything on the way?'

'He never says much.'

'You must have reached Cochin a few minutes after eight. What happened then?'

'We at once went into the patient's room together with the house-doctor on duty.'

'You spent the rest of the evening there?'

'No. The Professor stayed in the room about half an hour, watching for certain symptoms that did not develop. I told him he would do better to get some rest.'

'What time did he go up to the fourth floor?'

'I know that you have already asked these questions at the hospital.'

'The matron in charge told you?'

'It doesn't matter.'

'What time was it?'

'Not yet nine.'

'You didn't go up with him?'

'I stayed with the patient. It's a child.'

'I know. What time did the Professor come down again?'

'I went to warn him about eleven o'clock that what he'd been expecting had happened.'

'You went into the room where he was lying down?'

'Yes.'

'Was he dressed?'

'At the hospital he usually lies down fully dressed. He had merely taken off his jacket and undone his tie.'

'So you spent the whole of the time between eight-thirty and eleven at the patient's bedside. This being so, your chief could have walked down the stairs and left the hospital without your knowing?'

She must have been expecting it, for he had asked the same question at Cochin and someone would have warned her. In spite of that, he noticed her breasts rise and fall more rapidly. Had she prepared her reply in advance?

'That would have been impossible. For I went up at ten-fifteen to make sure there was nothing he wanted.'

Looking into her eyes, and putting much gentleness into his voice, Maigret remarked, without raising his tones:

'You're lying, aren't you?'

'Why do you say that?'

'Because I can feel that you are lying. Listen, Mademoiselle Decaux, it is easy for me to reconstruct, this very evening, your actions and movements at the hospital. Even if you have told the staff what to say, somebody can be found who will get flustered and reveal the truth. You did not go up before eleven o'clock.'

'The Professor did not leave the hospital.'

'How do you know?'

'Because I know him better than anyone does.'

She pointed to the evening paper lying on an occasional table.

'I picked it up from a table at Neuilly, and I've read it. Why did you let the young man go?'

She was referring to Pierrot, whose name he could see, upside-down, where he was sitting.

'You're so sure that he's not guilty?'

'I'm not sure about anything.'

'But you suspect the Professor of having murdered that girl?'

Instead of replying, he asked:

'You knew her?'

'You're forgetting that I am Monsieur Gouin's assistant. I was present when he operated on her.'

'You didn't like her?'

'Why should I have disliked her?'

As he had his pipe in his hand, she said:

'You may smoke. I don't mind.'

'Is it not true that you and the Professor had a more intimate relationship than the purely professional connexion?'

'They've told you that, too?'

She smiled, with a certain air of condescension.

'Are you very middle-class, Monsieur Maigret?'

'It depends on what you mean by that.'

'I am trying to find out whether you have preconceived ideas about conventional morality.'

'My dear, I've been in the police for nearly thirty-five years.'

'In that case, don't talk about intimate relations. There were intimate relations, but they were our working relations. The rest is of no importance.'

'You mean that there is no love between the two of you?'

'Certainly not in the sense that you give to the word. I admire Professor Gouin more than any other human being on earth. I do my best to help him. For ten or twelve hours on end, sometimes for longer, I am at his side and often he does not even notice it—so natural has our association become. It often happens that we spend the night waiting for symptoms to develop in a patient. When he operates in the provinces or abroad, I go with him. In the street I pay his taxis; I remind him of his appointments, and I telephone his wife to warn her that he won't be back.

'Long ago, in the beginning, there happened between us what usually occurs between a man and a woman constantly in close touch. He did not attach any importance to it. He has done the same with the nurses and with many other women.'

'You didn't attach any importance to it, either?'

'None.'

And she looked him straight in the eye as if challenging him to contradict her.

'You've never been in love?'

'With whom?'

'With any man. With the Professor.'

'Not in the sense that you give the word.'

'But you have devoted your life to him?'

'Yes.'

'Was it he who chose you as his assistant when you'd taken your degrees?'

'I am the one who applied. I'd had the idea in mind ever since I began to attend his lectures.'

'You said that in the beginning certain things happened between you. Am I to understand that they occur no longer?'

'You are a first-rate confessor, Monsieur Maigret. It still happens occasionally.'

'In your flat?'

'He's never set foot in here. I can't see him climbing four flights of stairs and entering these quarters.'

'At the hospital?'

'Sometimes. Sometimes also in his flat. You're overlooking that I also act as his secretary and that we often spend part of the day in the Avenue Carnot.'

'You know his wife well?'

'We are in touch practically every day.'

'What are your relations with her?'

He thought that Lucile's expression hardened a little.

'Indifferent,' she let fall.

'Mutually?'

'What are you trying to make me say?'

'The truth.'

'Let's say that Madame Gouin looks upon me in the same way as on her servants. Probably she does it to persuade herself that she is the Professor's wife. You've seen her?'

Once more Maigret forbore to reply.

'Why did your chief marry her?'

'Because he didn't want to be alone, I suppose.'

'It was before you became his assistant, wasn't it?'

'Several years before.'

'Does he get on well with her?'

'He is not the sort of man to quarrel with anyone, and he possesses an extraordinary capacity for failing to notice people.'

'Does he fail to notice his wife?'

'He eats a certain number of meals with her.'

'Is that all?'

'So far as I know.'

'Why do you think she married him?'

'She was only an insignificant nurse, remember. The Professor is reported to be a wealthy man.'

'Is he?'

'He makes a lot of money. He doesn't care about that.'

'But he's made a considerable fortune?'

She nodded in agreement and uncrossed her legs, taking care to draw the skirt of her dressing-gown round them.

'In short, in your view, he isn't happy in his marriage?'

'That's not quite right. His wife couldn't make him unhappy.'

'Nor Lulu?'

'Lulu, neither, that's my opinion.'

'If he wasn't in love with her, how do you explain that for more than two years . . .'

'I can't explain it to you. You must work it out for yourself.'

'Someone told me that he "had her under his skin".'

'Who?'

'Isn't it true?'

'It's true, and it's also false. She had become something that belonged to him.'

'But he wouldn't have sought a divorce in order to marry her?'

She looked at him, dumbfounded, and exclaimed:

'Never in the world! Besides, he would never have complicated his life with a divorce.'

'Not even to marry you?'

'He's never thought of it.'

'Have you?'

She blushed.

'Nor have I. What more would it have brought me? On the contrary, I should have lost in the bargain. You see, it is I who have had the better part, really. He does hardly anything without me. I share in his work. I know all about his books while he's actually writing them, and often I do his research for him. He never crosses Paris in a taxi unless I am at his side.'

'He is afraid of a sudden death?'

'Why do you ask that?'

She seemed surprised by the inspector's insight.

'For some years past it's true, more or less since he found out that his heart is not all it should be. At that time he consulted several of his colleagues. Perhaps you don't know, but most doctors are more terrified of illness than their patients.'

'I know.'

'He hasn't said anything to me on the subject, but he's gradually acquired the habit of never remaining alone.'

'If he had an attack in a taxi, for instance, what could you do?'

'Hardly anything. But I understand him.'

'In short, it is the idea of dying alone that terrifies him.'

'For what reason exactly did you come to see me, Inspector?'

'Perhaps in order not to bother your chief unnecessarily. His mistress was murdered on Monday night.'

'I don't like that word. It's inaccurate.'

'I use it in the sense it customarily has. Gouin had the material opportunity of committing the crime. As you admitted just now, he was alone on the fourth floor of the hospital from eight-forty-five until eleven. Nothing prevented him from walking out and driving to the Avenue Carnot.'

'If only you knew him, the notion that he could kill anyone would never occur to you.'

'Oh yes, it could have.'

His reply was so categorical that she looked at him in astonishment, without thinking of arguing.

'What do you mean?'

'You admit that his work, his career, his scientific research, his surgical and professional activity—put it how you will—is the only thing of value in his eyes?'

'To some extent.'

'To an extent much greater than in anyone else I have ever come across. Someone has applied to him the phrase "a force of nature".'

This time she did not ask who.

'Forces of nature are not concerned with the damage they may do. If, for one reason or another, Lulu had become a menace to his activities?'

'In what way could Lulu be a menace to the Professor?'

'You know that she was pregnant?'

'Did that alter the situation?'

She had not looked surprised.

'You knew?'

'The Professor spoke to me about it.'

'When?'

'Last Saturday.'

'You're sure it was last Saturday?'

'Absolutely. We were returning by taxi from the hospital. He told me, just as he tells me many things, without attaching any importance to it and rather as if he were talking to himself: "I think Louise is pregnant." '

'What was his expression?'

'None at all. A little ironical, as usual. You see, there are many things to which most people attach importance, but which have none for him.'

'What surprises me is that he should have told you on Saturday, whereas it was only on Monday evening, about six o'clock, that Lulu learnt the truth.'

'You forget he is a doctor, and was sleeping with her.'

'Do you think he also spoke to his wife about it?'

'It's unlikely.'

'Suppose Louise Filon had got it into her head that she wanted to marry him?'

'I don't think the idea ever occurred to her. Even in that case, he wouldn't have killed her. You're on the wrong track, Inspector. I don't maintain that you've let the guilty man go. For I don't see either, why Pierrot should have killed the girl.'

'In a passion, if she'd threatened not to see him any more.'

She shrugged her shoulders.

'You're very wide of the mark.'

'You have your own view?'

'I don't care to have one.'

He rose to empty his pipe into the grate, and automatically, as if he had been at home, he picked up the tongs to rearrange the logs.

'You're thinking of his wife?' he asked in a blank tone of voice, his back turned to her.

'I'm not thinking of anyone.'

'You don't like her?'

How could she have liked her? Germaine Gouin was a mere nurse, a fisherman's daughter, who had become overnight the Professor's legitimate wife, whereas Lucile Decaux, who had devoted her life to him and was trained to help him in his work, was only his assistant. Every evening when they came back from the hospital, she accompanied him out of the taxi, but it was to say good night on the threshold and to return to her own lodging in the Rue des Acacias, while he rode up in the lift to his wife.

'You suspect her, Mademoiselle Decaux?'

'I have never said that.'

'But it's in your thoughts.'

'I think that you don't hesitate to investigate the actions and movements of my chief on Monday evening, but that you aren't bothering about hers.'

'What do you know about that?'

'You've spoken to her?'

'I have at least found out, and it doesn't matter how, that she spent the evening with her sister. Do you know Antoinette?'

'Not personally. The Professor has mentioned her to me.'

'He doesn't like her?'

'It's she who hates him. He told me once that he always expects, whenever they accidentally meet, that she'll spit in his face.'

'You know nothing more about Madame Gouin?'

'Nothing,' she remarked curtly.

'Has she a lover?'

'Not to my knowledge. Besides, it's not my business.'

'Is she the kind of woman, supposing she were guilty, to let her husband be condemned in her place?'

As she was silent, Maigret could not help smiling.

'You must confess you wouldn't be annoyed if she had killed Lulu and we were able to prove it.'

'What I am sure about, is that the Professor didn't kill her.'

'Did he speak to you about the murder?'

'Not on Tuesday morning. He didn't know about it then. In the afternoon he told me incidentally that the police would probably be telephoning to ask for an appointment.'

'And since then?'

'He hasn't mentioned it.'

'Has he seemed upset by Lulu's death?'

'If it has affected him, he hasn't shown it. He's the same as he always is.'

'I suppose there's nothing else you have to tell me? Has he ever spoken of Pierre Eyraud, the musician?'

'Never.'

'Have you ever considered that he might have been jealous of him?'

'He's not a man to feel jealous of anybody.'

'Thank you very much, my dear, and forgive me for delaying your dinner. If you happen to remember any detail of interest, just give me a ring.'

'You won't be seeing my chief?'

'I don't know yet. Is he at home tonight?'

'It's the only free night in his week.'

'What will he be doing?'

'Working as usual. He has the proofs of his new book to read.'

Maigret sighed as he put on his overcoat.

'You're a funny sort of girl,' he murmured, almost to himself.

'There's nothing extraordinary about me.'

'Good night.'

'Good night, Monsieur Maigret.'

She accompanied him on to the landing and watched him walk downstairs. Outside, he found his black car, and the driver opened the door.

He almost gave him the Avenue Carnot address. Sooner or later he would have to decide on a *tête-à-tête* with Gouin. Why was he perpetually putting it off? He seemed to be circling round him, without daring to approach him, as if the personality of the Professor awed him.

'To the Quai!'

By this time, Etienne Gouin would be in the middle of dinner with his wife. Passing by, Maigret noticed that there were no lights in the right-hand side of the flat.

There was at least one point on which Lucile Decaux was wrong. Contrary to her statements, Gouin's conjugal relations were not so negative as she thought. The assistant maintained that her chief never talked about his business to his wife. On the other hand, Madame Gouin had provided the inspector with details of which only her husband could be the source.

Had he also told her that Lulu was pregnant?

He stopped the car a little higher up the Avenue in front of the *bistrot* where he had once before broken his journey to drink hot toddy. The wind was not so chill this evening, and he ordered a *marc*, although it was not the time for neat spirits, simply because it was the drink he had had the night before. At the Quai des Orfèvres they used to tease him about this peculiarity. If, for instance, he began an investigation on *calvados*, it was *calvados* throughout; the result was that there had been cases on beer, cases on red wine, and even a few on whisky.

He was on the point of telephoning his office to ask if there was anything new, and then of driving straight home. It was only because the telephone booth was occupied that he changed his mind.

On the way he did not utter a word.

'Will you still need me?' the driver asked when they had reached the courtyard of the P.J.

'You can take me to the Boulevard Lenoir in a few minutes. Unless you're due to go off duty.'

'I don't finish till eight.'

He went up and turned on the light in his

office; immediately the second door opened, disclosing Lucas.

'Inspector Janin telephoned. He is annoyed because no one told him that Pierrot had been found.'

Everybody had forgotten Janin, who had continued searching the La Chapelle district, until he had learnt from the newspapers that Maigret had interviewed the musician and let him go.

'He asks if he ought to keep his eye on him.'

'It's no longer worth it. Anything else?'

Lucas was opening his mouth to speak when the telephone rang. Maigret lifted the receiver.

'Inspector Maigret,' he announced frowning.

Suddenly Lucas realized that it was something important.

'Etienne Gouin here,' said the voice from the other end.

'Yes?'

'I understand you have just been questioning my assistant.'

Lucile Decaux had telephoned her chief to tell him all about it.

'So I have,' Maigret admitted.

'I should have thought it more correct, if you wanted information on my account, to apply direct to me.'

It seemed to Lucas that Maigret was a little dismayed and had to make an effort to regain his composure.

'It's a matter of opinion,' he replied rather shortly.

'You know where I live.'

'Very well. I shall come and see you.'

At the other end of the line there was a silence. The inspector heard indistinctly a woman's voice. Probably it was Madame Gouin saying something to her husband, who asked:

'When?'

'In an hour or an hour-and-a-half's time. I haven't eaten yet.'

'I shall expect you.'

Maigret was cut off.

'The Professor?' Lucas asked.

Maigret nodded.

'What does he want?'

'He wants to be interviewed. Are you free?'

'To go down there with you?'

'Yes. But first we'll go and have a bite.'

They did so in the Place Dauphine, at the table where the inspector had lunched and dined so often that it was known as Maigret's table.

Throughout the meal, he never uttered a word.

8

IN the course of his career Maigret had interviewed thousands of people—perhaps tens of
thousands—some of them men of considerable
position, others who were more famous for their
wealth, and others still who were reckoned among
the cleverest of international crooks.

Nevertheless he attached an importance to this
coming interview that he had never ascribed to
any that had gone before, and it was not Gouin's
social position that impressed him, nor the re-
nown he enjoyed throughout the world.

He was well aware that ever since the beginning of the case, Lucas had been wondering why
he had not fairly and squarely put a few searching questions to the Professor, and even now
poor Lucas was nonplussed by his chief's bad
temper.

Maigret could not admit the truth to him, nor

to anyone else—even to his wife. In fact, he hardly dared to formulate it precisely in his own mind.

He was impressed, it is true, by what he knew of Gouin and what he had found out. But for a reason that no one, very likely, could have guessed.

Like the Professor, Maigret had been born in a little village in central France, and, like him, from his earliest years he had been thrown on his own resources.

Had not Maigret started to study medicine? If he had been in a position to continue his studies, he would probably not have become a surgeon, for lack of the necessary manual dexterity, but he had an idea, none the less, that he and Lulu's lover had some characteristics in common.

It was vain of him, and that is why he preferred not to think of it. But they both possessed, so it seemed to him, a comparable knowledge of life and of mankind.

By no means the same, and above all not the same reactions. They were, as it might be, opposites, but opposites of equal value.

What he knew of Gouin he had learnt through the words and attitudes of five different women. All he had seen of him had been his outline on the pavement of the Avenue Carnot and a photograph over a chimney-piece; and certainly the most revealing incident had been Janvier's short telephone account of the Professor's appearance in Louise Filon's flat.

He was now going to find out whether he was

wrong. He had prepared himself for the interview to the best of his ability, and if he was taking Lucas with him it was not for the sake of his help, but to give the occasion a more official air, and perhaps to remind himself that he was going to the Avenue Carnot in his capacity as an Inspector of the P.J. and not simply as a man interested in another human being.

He had drunk wine with his dinner. When the waiter had asked him if he wanted brandy or a liqueur, he had ordered an old *marc de Bourgogne*, with the result that he was feeling a certain warmth within him as he drove along in the car.

The Avenue Carnot was quiet and deserted, with subdued lights showing through the curtains of the flats. When he passed by the lodge, he thought the concierge looked at him with a reproachful expression.

The two men took the lift, and the house around seemed hushed and turned in upon itself and its secrets.

It was eight-forty when Maigret pulled the shining brass handle that worked the electric bell; steps were heard inside and a young, rather pretty, maid, wearing a smart apron over her black uniform, opened the door and said:

'If the gentlemen would like to take off their coats . . .'

He had wondered whether Gouin would receive them in the sitting-room, in the more or less family part of the flat. He did not at once get an answer. The maid hung up their coats in

161

a cupboard, left the visitors in the hall, and disappeared.

She did not return, but Gouin wasted no time in presenting himself; here he seemed taller and thinner than in the street. He scarcely glanced at them and did no more than to murmur:

'Would you kindly come this way . . .'

He preceded them down a corridor leading to his library. The walls were almost entirely lined with bound volumes. The room was suffused with a soft light, and logs were burning in a fireplace much grander than Lucile Decaux's.

'Please sit down.'

He indicated some chairs, and took one himself. All this was of no account. So far the two men had not looked at each other. Lucas, who felt himself one too many, was made even more uncomfortable by the fact that the chair was too deep for his short legs, and he was sitting too near the fire.

'I had expected that you would come alone.'

Maigret introduced his colleague.

'I brought Sergeant Lucas who will take shorthand notes.'

It was at this moment that their eyes for the first time crossed, and Maigret thought he read in the Professor's something like a reproach. Perhaps there was also, though he could not be sure of this, a certain disappointment. It was difficult to say because, outwardly, Gouin seemed ordinary enough. Actors at the theatre, and specially operatic basses, are often of his kind of

162

large-boned build, with strongly chiselled features and pouches under the eyes.

His eyes were small and pale, and without any particular brilliance, but in his glance there was an uncommon power of penetration.

While this glance rested upon him, Maigret could have sworn that Gouin was as curious about him as he was about the Professor.

Did he, too, find him more ordinary than he had imagined?

Lucas had taken a notebook and pencil out of his pocket, and this kept him in countenance.

It was impossible to forecast what tone the conversation would take, and Maigret was careful to hold his peace and wait.

'Do you not think, Monsieur Maigret, that it would have been more rational to apply to me in the first instance instead of bothering that poor girl?'

He was speaking naturally, in unemphatic tones, as if he were talking of quite ordinary things.

'You are referring to Mademoiselle Decaux? She didn't seem to me to be in the least upset. I suppose that as soon as I left her she telephoned to tell you all about it?'

'She reported your questions and her replies. She thought it was important. Women are everlastingly anxious to convince themselves of their importance.'

'Lucile Decaux is your closest colleague, isn't she?'

'She is my assistant.'

'Doesn't she also act as your secretary?'

'She does. And as she must have told you, she follows me about wherever I go. That gives her the impression that she plays a major part in my life.'

'She is in love with you?'

'As she would be with whatever chief she had, provided he were famous.'

'She seemed to me devoted to you, up to the point of committing perjury, if need be, in order to get you out of a difficulty.'

'She would do so without a moment's hesitation. My wife has also been in touch with you.'

'She told you?'

'Just like Lucile, she has given me the fullest details of your conversation.'

He spoke of his wife in the same detached way in which he had referred to his assistant. There was no warmth in his voice. He was stating facts, without attaching any sentimental importance to them.

People of no account who came into contact with him probably went into rhapsodies over his directness of manner, and he had in fact no pose about him; he was not in the least concerned with the effect he produced on others.

It is very rarely one meets human beings who are not playing a part, even when they are alone with themselves. Most men experience a need to observe themselves living and hear themselves speaking.

Not so with Gouin. He was completely himself and he took no trouble to conceal his feelings.

When he had spoken of Lucile Decaux, he had meant by his words and his attitude:

'What she takes for devotion is really only a kind of vanity, a need to consider herself exceptional. Any one of my women students would do the same as she does. Thus, she makes her life seem interesting to herself, and probably imagines that I owe her a debt of gratitude.'

If he was not explicit, it was because he judged Maigret capable of understanding, and spoke to him as to an equal.

'I have not yet told you why I telephoned you this evening and asked you to call. But in any case, please note that I wanted to meet you.'

He was a man, and he was sincere. Since they had met face to face, he had been incessantly watching the inspector and had not concealed it, observing him as if he were a specimen of humanity whom he wished to know better.

'While my wife and I were at dinner, I had a telephone call. It was from someone you know already, from the Madame Brault who was Louise's charwoman.'

He did not say Lulu, but Louise, referring to her as simply as he had to the others, well understanding that it was superfluous to offer explanations.

'Madame Brault has got it into her head that she has grounds for blackmailing me. She did not beat about the bush, although I did not at once understand her first remark. She said:

' "I have the revolver, Monsieur Gouin."

'To begin with, I wondered what revolver she meant.'

'May I ask a question?'

'Please do.'

'Have you ever met Madame Brault?'

'I don't think so. Louise has spoken to me about her. She knew her before she moved in here. Apparently she is a strange creature who has many times been to prison. As she only worked in the flat in the mornings, and I hardly ever had occasion to call there at that time, I do not remember having met her. Though I may have passed her on the stairs.'

'Please go on.'

'She told me that when she went into the sitting-room on Monday morning, she found the revolver on the table and . . .'

'Did she say specifically: on the table?'

'Yes. She added that she had hidden it on the landing, in a flowerpot that contains an evergreen plant. Your men must have searched the flat without thinking of looking outside it.'

'It was ingenious on her part.'

'In short, she claims now to be in possession of the revolver and for a considerable sum would be willing to let me have it back.'

'Have it *back*?'

'It belongs to me.'

'How you know?'

'She gave me a description, including the serial number.'

'Have you had this weapon for long?'

'Eight or nine years. I had gone to Belgium to operate. At that time I travelled more than I do now. It has even happened that I have been called to go as far afield as the United States and India. My wife often told me that she was afraid to be alone in the house for days on end, and sometimes for several weeks. At the hotel where I was staying, in Liège, some locally manufactured guns were on exhibition in a glass-case. It occurred to me to buy a small automatic. I ought to add that I did not declare it to the Customs.'

Maigret smiled.

'What room was it kept in?'

'In a drawer in my desk. That's where I saw it last, some months ago. I have never made use of it. I had completely forgotten it when I received this telephone call.'

'What did you say to Madame Brault?'

'That I would give her an answer later.'

'When?'

'Probably this evening. It was then that I telephoned you.'

'Will you go down there, Lucas? You have the address?'

'Yes, Chief.'

Lucas was obviously delighted to escape from the heavy atmosphere of the room, for though the two men were talking in low tones and apparently saying quite ordinary things, a veiled tension could be distinctly felt.

'Can you find your overcoat? Would you like me to ring for the maid?'

'I can find it, thank you.'

167

After the door had shut, they were silent for a moment. It was Maigret who spoke first.

'Is your wife aware of this?'

'Of Madame Brault's blackmail?'

'Yes.'

'She heard what I said on the telephone, for I took the call in the dining-room. I told her the rest.'

'What was her reaction?'

'She advised me to come to terms.'

'Have you wondered why?'

'Well now, Monsieur Maigret, whether it is my wife, Lucile Decaux, or any of the others—they all derive a deep satisfaction from persuading themselves that they are devoted to me. In short, it is a question of which of them can help and protect me best.'

There was no irony in his words. Wholly without acrimony, he was dissecting their states of mind with the same detachment as he would have brought to the dissection of a body.

'Why do you suppose my wife felt the need to go down to talk to you? In order to cast herself in the role of a wife protecting the work and peace of mind of her husband.'

'Isn't that really the case?'

He looked at Maigret without replying.

'Your wife seemed to me, Professor, to be exhibiting for you a sort of understanding that is pretty rare.'

'True enough, she maintains that she is not jealous.'

'But it is only a pretence?'

'That depends on the meaning you give to the word. It probably is a matter of indifference to her whether I sleep with other people.'

'Even with Louise Filon?'

'Yes, at the start. Don't forget that Germaine, who was only an insignificant nurse, became Madame Gouin overnight.'

'Were you in love with her?'

'No.'

'Why did you marry her?'

'To have someone in the house. The old woman who looked after me had not much longer to live. I do not like being alone, Monsieur Maigret. I do not know if you have experienced that feeling?'

'Perhaps you also like the people around yourself to owe everything to you?'

He did not object. On the contrary the remark seemed to have pleased him.

'In a sense, yes.'

'Was it for that reason that you chose a girl of modest family?'

'The others exasperate me.'

'She knew what to expect when she married you?'

'Very precisely.'

'At what moment did she begin to make herself unpleasant?'

'She has never made herself unpleasant. You have seen her. She is admirable, takes excellent care of the house and never insists on my taking her out for an evening or inviting friends to dinner.'

169

'If I understand it rightly, she spends her days waiting for you.'

'More or less. It is enough for her to be Madame Gouin and to know that one day she will be Etienne Gouin's widow.'

'You think she's self-seeking?'

'Let us put it that she will not be sorry to have at her disposal the fortune I shall leave her. At this minute I am prepared to bet that she is listening behind the door. She was worried when I telephoned you. She would have preferred me to receive you in the sitting-room with her present.'

He had not lowered his voice when he declared that Germaine was listening behind the door, and Maigret could have sworn that he heard a slight noise in the adjoining room.

'According to her, it was she who suggested installing Louise Filon in this house.'

'So she did. I had not thought of it. I did not even know that a flat was vacant.'

'Didn't this arrangement seem strange to you?'

'Why should it?'

The question had surprised him.

'Were you in love with Louise?'

'Now, listen, Monsieur Maigret, that is the second time you have used that word. In medicine we do not recognize it.'

'You needed her?'

'Physically, yes. Do I have to explain? I am sixty-two years old.'

'I know.'

'That's all there is to it.'

'You weren't jealous of Pierrot?'

'I would rather he had not existed.'

As he had done at Lucile Decaux's, Maigret rose to rearrange a log that had slipped. He was thirsty. The Professor had not thought of offering him a drink. The *marc* he had drunk after dinner furred his mouth, and he had been smoking continuously.

'Have you met him?' he asked.

'Who?'

'Pierrot.'

'Once. Usually they both contrived that it should not happen.'

'What were Lulu's feelings towards you?'

'What feelings do you suppose she would have? I imagine you know her story. Naturally, she spoke to me of gratitude and affection. The truth is simpler. She had no desire to be poor again. You ought to know that. People who have really gone hungry, and suffered poverty in the darkest sense of the word, and who have managed in one way or another to climb out of it, are willing to do anything in the world to avoid falling back into their former life.'

It was true, as Maigret was in a good position to know.

'Was she in love with Pierrot?'

'If you insist on the words!' the Professor sighed resignedly. 'She needed some sentimental interest in her life. She also needed to create problems for herself. I said just now that women like to feel themselves important. Because of that, I suppose, they have to complicate their lives, perplex themselves and constantly imagine that a choice lies before them.'

'A choice between what?' Maigret asked, with the shadow of a smile, to oblige the speaker to be more precise.

'Louise thought that she had a choice between her musician and myself.'

'And she hadn't?'

'Not in reality. I have told you why.'

'Did she ever threaten to leave you?'

'She sometimes claimed to be thinking it over.'

'But you weren't afraid that it would happen?'

'No.'

'She didn't try, either, to persuade you to marry her?'

'Her ambition didn't rise so high as that. I am convinced that she would have been a little alarmed of becoming Madame Gouin. What she needed was security. A flat with heating, three meals a day, and decent clothes.'

'What would have happened if you had disappeared?'

'I had taken out a life-assurance in her favour.'

'Have you also taken one out in favour of Lucile Decaux?'

'No. There is no point. When I die, she will attach herself to my successor as she has done to me, and nothing will change in her life.'

They were interrupted by the telephone bell. Gouin was about to get up to reply when he stopped:

'That will be your detective.'

It was indeed Lucas, speaking from the Batignolles police station, the nearest to Madame Brault's home.

'I have the weapon, sir. She pretended at first that she didn't know what I was talking about.'

'What have you done with her?'

'She's with me, here.'

'Have her sent to the Quai. Where did she find the revolver?'

'She maintains it was on the table.'

'Why did she decide that it belonged to the Professor?'

'According to her, it was obvious. She won't give any details. She is furiously angry, and tried to scratch my face. What does he have to say?'

'Nothing definite. We are having a talk.'

'Shall I join you?'

'Go to the laboratory first to make sure there are no finger-prints on the automatic. That will enable you to take your prisoner along with you to the Quai.'

'Very good, sir,' Lucas sighed, without enthusiasm.

Only now did Gouin think of offering him a drink.

'Will you have a brandy?'

'Gladly.'

He rang. The maid who had let Maigret and Lucas in appeared at once.

'The *fine!*'

They did not speak while they were waiting. When the maid came back, there was only one glass on the tray.

'Forgive me, but I never drink,' the Professor said, leaving Maigret to help himself.

It was probably not on principle, nor for reasons of diet, but simply because he did not need it.

9

MAIGRET took his time. Glass in hand, he gazed at the Professor, who calmly returned his gaze.

'The concierge, too, owes you a debt of gratitude, doesn't she? Unless I'm wrong, you saved her son?'

'I don't expect gratitude from anybody.'

'She is none the less devoted to you, and like Lucile Decaux is ready to tell lies to get you out of trouble.'

'Quite so. It is always pleasant to think of oneself as heroic.'

'Don't you sometimes feel alone in the world as you conceive it?'

'Human beings are always alone, whatever they may think. It is enough to admit it once and for all, and to adapt oneself accordingly.'

'I thought you had a horror of being alone?'

'That is not the kind of solitude I had in mind. Let us say, if you like, that I find it distressing to have emptiness around me. I do not like to be alone in a flat, in the street, or in a car. But that is a matter of physical loneliness, not solitude of mind.'

'You are afraid of death?'

'The thought of being dead does not disturb me. But I hate the act of dying and all that goes with it. In your profession, Inspector, you have witnessed death almost as often as I have.'

He understood very well that this was his weak point, and that his fear of dying alone was the little touch of human cowardice that made him a man like any other. Nor was he ashamed of it.

'Since my last heart attack, someone has nearly always been with me. Medically, there is no point in it. However, though it may seem odd, anybody's presence is reassuring. Once when I was about in town, and suddenly felt slightly faint, I went into the first bar I came to.'

It was at this moment that Maigret sprang the question he had long been holding in reserve.

'What was your reaction when you observed that Louise was pregnant?'

He seemed surprised, not that this fact was mentioned, but that it might be considered as a possible complication.

'None,' was all he said.

'Didn't she speak to you about it?'

'No. I suppose she didn't know.'

'She found out about six on Monday. You saw her later. She didn't mention it?'

'All she said was that she didn't feel well, and was going to lie down.'

'Did you think that the child was yours?'

'I never gave it a thought.'

'You've never had children?'

'Not to my knowledge.'

'Have you never wanted one?'

His reply shocked Maigret, who for thirty years had very much wanted to be a father.

'*For what reason?*' the Professor demanded.

'Surely!'

'What do you mean?'

'Nothing.'

'Some people, with no serious interests in life, imagine that a child will give them importance and a sort of value; that they will thus have something to leave behind them. It is not so in my case.'

'Don't you think that, given your age and her lover's, Lulu would have decided that the child was his?'

'Scientifically, there is nothing in it.'

'I am speaking of what she may have thought.'

'It is possible.'

'Wouldn't that be enough for her to make up her mind to leave you for Pierrot?'

He did not hesitate.

'No,' he replied, like a man certain of possessing the truth. 'She would certainly have sworn to me that the child was mine.'

'Would you have recognized it?'

'Why not?'

'Even though you doubted whether you were the father?'

'What difference does that make? One child is as good as another.'

'Would you have married the mother?'

'I see no reason for it.'

'In your opinion, she would not have tried to make you marry her?'

'If she had tried, she would not have succeeded.'

'Because you do not wish to give up your wife?'

'Simply because I find these complications ridiculous. I am answering frankly, because I think you are capable of understanding me.'

'Have you spoken to your wife about it?'

'On Sunday afternoon, if I remember rightly. Yes, it was Sunday. I spent part of the afternoon at home.'

'Why did you tell your wife about it?'

'I also told my assistant.'

'I know.'

'Well, then?'

He was right in thinking that Maigret understood. There was something terribly disdainful and at the same time tragic, in the way in which the Professor spoke of people around him, or rather of the women around him. He took them at their own value, without any illusions, and asked from each only what she could give him. In his eyes it was as if they were little more than inanimate objects.

He did not even take the trouble to hold his tongue in their presence. For what difference did it make? He could think aloud, without bothering about their reactions, still less about what their thoughts or sentiments might be.

'What did your wife say?'

'She asked me what I intended to do.'

'And you replied that you would recognize the child?'

He nodded.

'It did not occur to you that this avowal of yours might cause her some anxiety?'

'Perhaps.'

This time Maigret thought he noticed in the speaker something he had not perceived up to then, or that he had not been able to fathom. There had seemed to be a note of private satisfaction in the Professor's voice as he said *'Perhaps.'*

'You did it on purpose?' he attacked.

'Telling her about it?'

Maigret was sure that Gouin would have preferred not to smile and to have remained impassive, but his feelings were stronger than he was, and for the first time his lips parted curiously.

'In short, you were not sorry to upset your wife, nor your assistant?'

Gouin's silence amounted to an assent.

'Might not one of them have conceived the idea of putting Louise Filon out of the way?'

'The idea must long since have occurred to them. They both hated Louise. I know of no one

179

who has not at some time wished for the death of another person. But people capable of putting these ideas into execution are rare. Luckily for you!'

All this was true. And that indeed was the preposterous thing about this conversation. Everything the Professor had said from the start, Maigret himself believed deep within him. Their ideas about men and their motives were not very far apart.

The difference lay in the attitudes with which they faced the problem.

Gouin only made use of what Maigret would have called pure reason. Whereas the inspector was trying . . .

He would have been hard put to it to define what he was trying to do. Perhaps from understanding people he derived not merely a feeling of pity, but also a kind of affection.

Gouin observed them from on high.

Maigret placed himself on the same level as they.

'Louise Filon has been murdered,' he said slowly.

'That is the fact. Someone has gone to the very limit.'

'Have you wondered who it might be?'

'That is your job, not mine.'

'Have you considered that it might be yourself?'

'Of course. Before I knew that my wife had spoken to you, I was surprised that you did not come and interview me. The concierge had warned me that people had been talking to you about me.'

She, too! And Gouin accepted it as his natural due.

'You went to Cochin on Monday evening, but you only stayed half an hour at your patient's beside.'

'I went upstairs to lie down in a room on the fourth floor that is kept at my disposal.'

'You were alone, and there was nothing to stop you from leaving the hospital without being seen, coming here by taxi and then returning to your room.'

'At what time, do you think, these comings and goings could have taken place?'

'It has to be between nine o'clock and eleven.'

'What time was Pierre Eyraud in Louise's flat?'

'At a quarter to ten.'

'So that I should have had to kill Louise some time after that?'

Maigret assented.

'Given the time necessary for the journey, I could not have been back at the hospital between ten and ten-thirty.'

Maigret worked it out in his mind. The Professor's reasoning was sound. Of a sudden, Maigret felt disillusioned. Something was not happening as he had foreseen. He knew what was to follow, and hardly paid attention to the speaker's words.

'The fact is, Monsieur Maigret, that at five past

ten one of my colleagues, Dr. Lanvin, who had been seeing a patient on the third floor, came up to see me. He did not quite trust his own diagnosis. He asked me to accompany him. I went down to the third floor. Neither my assistant, nor my staff, could have told you about this, for they knew nothing about it.

'This is not the testimony of an anxious woman, but of five or six people, among whom was the patient, who had never previously seen me and probably does not know my name.'

'I never thought that you had killed Lulu.'

He made a point of calling her by this name, which seemed to annoy the Professor. He, too, was experiencing the need to be cruel.

'I merely expected that you would try to cover up for the person who did kill her.'

Gouin showed that the shot had gone home. A slight flush rose to his cheeks, and for an instant his eyes turned away from the inspector's.

Someone rang the doorbell. It was Lucas, carrying a small parcel, whom the maid showed into the room.

'No finger-prints,' he said, unwrapping the weapon and handing it to his chief.

He glanced from one to the other, surprised by the prevailing calm, and by the fact that they were still in the same places and in the same attitudes, as if while he had been running about Paris, time had stood still in the library.

'Is this your revolver, Monsieur Gouin?'

It was a toy-like weapon, with a nickel-plated barrel and a butt in mother-of-pearl; if the shot had not been fired point-blank, it would probably not have done much harm.

'One bullet is missing from the magazine,' Lucas explained. 'I telephoned Gastine-Renette, who will supply the usual tests tomorrow. But he is already convinced that this is the weapon from which the shot was fired on Monday.'

'I suppose, Monsieur Gouin, that your wife, like your assistant, had access to your desk-drawer? It wasn't kept locked?'

'I never lock up anything.'

This, too, came from a kind of contempt for people. He had nothing to hide. It mattered little to him, if others read his private papers.

'Weren't you surprised on Monday evening when you came in to find your sister-in-law in the flat?'

'She generally tries to avoid me.'

'I think she, at least, detests you, doesn't she?'

'That is merely another way of making her life seem interesting.'

'Your wife told me that her sister had called by chance, because she happened to be in the neighbourhood.'

'It could be.'

'When I questioned Antoinette, she told me that her sister had telephoned her to ask her to come round.'

Gouin was listening attentively, without displaying any perceptible emotions. Lying back in his chair, with his legs crossed, he had interlaced his fingers, and Maigret was struck by their length, as slender as a pianist's.

'Sit down, Lucas.'

'Shall I get a drink for your detective?'

Lucas shook his head.

'There is another statement of your wife's which I should like to have confirmed, and only you can do so.'

The Professor motioned that he was waiting.

'Some time ago you had a heart attack when you were in Lulu's flat.'

'That's right. A little exaggerated, but true.'

'Is it also true that your distracted mistress called in your wife?'

Gouin seemed surprised.

'Who told you that?'

'It doesn't matter. But is it true?'

'Not entirely.'

'You realize that your reply is of enormous importance.'

'I realize it from the manner in which you are putting the question, but I do not know why. I did not feel well on that particular night. I asked Louise to go upstairs and fetch a medicine bottle that is kept in my bathroom. She did so. My wife opened the door for her, for the servants had gone to bed, and their bedrooms are on the sixth floor. My wife, who was in bed, too, when Louise came, went to find the bottle.'

'Did they come down together?'

'Yes. But, in the meantime, the attack had

passed and I had already left the third-floor flat. I had just walked through the door when Louise and my wife appeared, both in nightgowns.'

'Allow me, a moment.'

Maigret said a few words in a low voice to Lucas, who left the room. Gouin asked no questions and did not seem surprised.

'Was the door wide open, behind you?'

'No. It was pulled to.'

Maigret would have preferred him to tell a lie. For the last hour he would have liked to see Gouin attempting to tell an untruth, but he was a man of relentless sincerity.

'You are sure?'

He was giving him a last chance.

'Absolutely.'

'To your knowledge your wife has never been to see Lulu in her third-floor flat?'

'You little know her.'

Had not Germaine Gouin stated that this was the sole occasion on which she had previously been in the flat?

Now, in fact, she had not entered it on that night. Yet, when she had come down to see the inspector, she had not cast a single curious glance around her, and had behaved as if the place were well known to her.

That was her second lie, to which ought to be added that she had not mentioned the fact that Lulu was pregnant.

'Do you think she is still eavesdropping at the door?'

Sending Lucas to post himself in the vestibule of the flat had been a needless precaution.

'I am convinced she is . . .' the Professor began.

And the communicating door immediately opened. Madame Gouin took a few steps forward into the room, just enough to be able to look her husband in the face, and never had Maigret seen in human eyes so much hatred and contempt. The Professor did not turn away, but received the impact without flinching.

The inspector rose to his feet.

'I am compelled to place you under arrest, Madame Gouin.'

Almost absent-mindedly, and still turned towards her husband, she said:

'I know.'

'I suppose you have heard everything?'

'Yes.'

'You admit that you killed Louise Filon?'

She nodded, looking as if she were about to throw herself like a fury upon the man who was still meeting her gaze.

'He knew that this would happen,' she announced at length, in a jerky voice, while her breast rapidly rose and fell. 'I wonder now whether it is not what he really wanted, if it was not consciously and in order to egg me on, that he told me certain things.'

'You called your sister in order to provide yourself with an alibi?'

Again she nodded assent. Maigret continued:

'I suppose you went downstairs when you left

186

the dressing-room on the pretext of preparing hot toddy?'

He saw her begin to frown, and she turned her glance away from Gouin to level it at the inspector. She seemed to hesitate. One could feel she was waging a battle with herself. At length she uttered:

'That is not true.'

'What is not true?'

'That my sister stayed here alone.'

In Gouin's eyes there flashed an ironic expression. Maigret coloured, for this expression clearly meant:

'What did I tell you?'

And it was true that Germaine was not willing to bear the whole weight of the crime. She had only to remain silent. But she was talking.

'Antoinette knew what I was going to do. As at the last moment I did not have enough courage, she came downstairs with me.'

'Did she go in?'

'She remained on the stairs.'

And after a pause, with an air of defying the world, she added:

'So much the worse. It is the truth.'

Her lips were trembling with stifled anger.

'Now he can set about renewing his harem!'

*

Madame Gouin was wrong. Little change took place in the Professor's life. A few months later Lucile Decaux came to live with him, while continuing to serve as his secretary and assistant.

If she tried to get him to marry her, Maigret
never knew.

In any event, the Professor did not remarry.

And when his name turns up in conversation,
Maigret pretends not to hear it, or quickly changes
the subject.

Shadow Rock Farm,
Lakeville, Conn.
31 August, 1953